Yours from the Tower

Also by Sally Nicholls

All Fall Down

Season of Secrets

The Silent Stars Go By

Things a Bright Girl Can Do

PRAISE FOR *YOURS FROM THE TOWER*

'I loved this book. An unputdownable friendship story told in letters so vivid and immersive that I felt like joining in with the correspondence'
Hilary McKay

'An addictive, romantic epistolary novel'
Guardian

'This immersive, uplifting book is an absolute delight'
Irish Times

'The novel is heart-warming, intelligent and exciting, and thoroughly recommended for girls (and boys) hovering on the cusp of adolescence. I loved it'
Literary Review

'Nicholls' award-winning young adult novels conjure up the confusion and passion of adolescence – and never more so than in this thrilling and cleverly constructed story . . . Against a backdrop of feminism, Nicholls balances their contrasting characters with delightful wit and warmth'
Daily Mail

'Fans of historical fiction will delight in the latest YA title from Sally Nicholls'
The Oldie

'A gorgeous, immersive book'
Observer

'This YA romantic comedy is so much darn fun . . . with honesty, warmth and oodles of humour'
Irish Independent

'With great affection and sympathy, these winning heroines forge their own paths in this highly readable, tautly paced work'
***Publishers Weekly*, starred review**

'A breath of fresh air . . . Sally Nicholls' latest historical novel *Yours from the Tower* is a rewarding read for youngsters that never feels like a dull lesson'
Daily Telegraph

'A warm, gentle work with well-drawn characters and brisk pacing celebrating female friendship and independence'
Kirkus

'The perfect novel for our anxiety-ridden times, with its thrilling plot, brave heroines and empowering message . . . This is simply a heavenly book'
***The Bookseller*, 'Book of the Month'**

'Technically brilliant and consistently engaging . . . could well be [Sally Nicholls'] best yet'
Books for Keeps

THE SILENT STARS GO BY

'Sally Nicholls conjures another era with a miraculous lightness of touch that fills me with joy and envy'
Frances Hardinge

THINGS A BRIGHT GIRL CAN DO

Shortlisted for the Carnegie Medal, National Book Award, Books Are My Bag Readers Award and the YA Book Prize

'Nicholls has brought alive the young women of the past to empower the next generation'
The Times

Yours from the Tower

SALLY NICHOLLS

ANDERSEN PRESS

This paperback edition first published in 2024 by
Andersen Press Limited
20 Vauxhall Bridge Road, London SW1V 2SA, UK
Vijverlaan 48, 3062 HL Rotterdam, Nederland
www.andersenpress.co.uk

First published in hardback in 2023 by Andersen Press Ltd

2 4 6 8 10 9 7 5 3 1

British Library Cataloguing in Publication Data available.

ISBN 978 1 83913 481 4

Printed and bound in China

MIX
Paper from
responsible sources
FSC® C104723

Another one for Nicola,
Carolyn and Sarah.

Bannon House
Abyford
Perthshire
20th November 1896

Dear Polly and Sophia,

Girls, please write to me at once and tell me how you are. I am so lonely I could die. I have been at my grandmother's house for FOUR MONTHS now and absolutely NOTHING has happened. Grandmother sees nobody, visits nobody, goes nowhere. I am expected to wait upon her hand and foot – fetch her smelling salts, take her letters to the post, read aloud to her, take dictation. I am absolutely wretched.

I know she does not intend for me to marry. She said to me, 'So nice to have a granddaughter to keep house. Much more suitable than a paid companion. It has been so lonely since your aunt Lucy passed on.' I do not keep house, though. Her housekeeper, Sarah, does everything and always has done. I tried ordering food when I first came here – I got the big book of recipes down from the kitchen shelf and looked through it, trying to find interesting things to eat. But Sarah and Grandmother soon put me in my place. 'We have chop on Monday,' said Sarah. 'And mutton on Tuesday. And on Wednesdays, your grandmother is partial to Irish stew.' She went on like this through all the days of the week. And that was that! I am not a housekeeper. I am basically a chattel.

I cannot quite believe I am saying this, but I would give anything to be back at school with you all. Even needlework class and gymnastics would be better than a small Scottish village in the middle of nowhere! Oh, to be walking down to the grocer's with Polly on one arm and Sophia on the other. Oh, to lie in our bedroom giggling together after Lights Out. Oh, to have someone to talk to who is not Grandmother or the servants! Sixteen years my aunt Lucy lived here! I think I shall die of boredom.

Sophia, write and tell me *everything* about the Season. Have you met any handsome men yet? Are you in love? How I wish *I* had an aunt who was an aristocrat! Please, marry a baronet for my sake and tell him you cannot be parted from your beloved Tirzah. You could employ me as your hermit. I would be perfectly happy to sit in a grotto in the grounds of your castle, spouting riddles for the visiting gentry. I would see more life there than I do here. Polly, tell me about all your brothers and sisters. How is working life? Do you go to many dances in Liverpool?

My arm is tired with all this writing. I've been thinking – all this time, I've written you a letter apiece, and I've mostly written the same thing in each of them. But now you've gone to London, Sophia, I suppose you won't have much time for letter writing. Why don't we just write each other one letter apiece? I am going to put this one in an envelope addressed to Sophia, and then Sophia, when you write back, write a letter to both of us and post it to Polly in an envelope with my letter inside. Do you see? That way we need only write one letter each. I cannot separate the two of you in my head anyway. I think of us always as a trio, all cuddled up together in our little dorm at school. Oh, I miss you both so much! Please say you'll fall in with my scheme. It will make me feel like you're not so far away.

Your sister in misery and exile,

Tirzah

12 Wimpole Street
Mayfair
London
24th November 1896

Dear Polly and Tirzah,

Firstly – my aunt Eliza is not an aristocrat. She just married my uncle Simon, who is the younger son of a baron and therefore an Honourable – which means his father was an aristocrat, I suppose. My aunt Eliza is decidedly middle class, and she's horribly aware of it. She is always talking about 'darling Grandpapa's house', and poor Uncle Simon looks frightfully sick whenever she does so. He doesn't like to tell her that it's not the done thing to call your in-laws 'Grandpapa' or boast about your country houses. She is not very pleased about me being here in my homemade ballgowns, looking so obviously the poor relation. She keeps talking about her darling sister who made a rather *unfortunate* match to a drawing master. I do call it unkind. I would rather marry a pauper than Uncle Simon. And Daddy isn't a drawing master anyway. He's a painter. It's not his fault his paintings aren't the sort that sell.

I suppose I should be grateful to Aunt Eliza for paying my school fees and letting me come and stay with her for the Season (though my cousins Mariah and Isabelle rather sneer at me for having gone to school – *they* had governesses, of course). And it *is* fun – all the balls and tea parties and so forth. The other girls are rather jolly, even if they *are* fearful snobs. Isabelle and Mariah certainly are. I think it's being brought up by Aunt Eliza that does it. They all treat me rather as a hired monkey – 'Sophia, fetch me my slippers, would you?' 'Sophia, tell Langton to get the coach ready for seven.' I think your grandmother and my aunt would get along, Tirzah!

Mariah and Isabelle are just jealous because the men like me more than them. I danced every dance at Lady Frances's ball on Saturday, and weren't they green? They cannot understand it – a plain little thing like me. But men like a girl who makes them laugh.

No, I have *not* fallen in love yet – though I certainly intend to be married before the end of the Season. I won't get more than one Season, so I shall make the most of it.

Tell me, Polly – how are you coping in that orphanage of yours? Do you still like being a schoolmarm?

Your dear friend,

The not-yet-titled Sophia

45 Park Lane
Liverpool
27th November 1896

Dear Sophia and Tirzah,

It feels very strange to be writing to you both at once like this – it's so queer to be copying all my questions to Sophia onto your letter, Tirzah. But I do rather like it. I miss you both enormously, although I like being at home too. I love my home. It isn't as grand as Sophia's aunt's house in Mayfair. The carpet is flapping off the top of the stairs, and there are greasy fingerprints all along the walls, and it's draughty and shabby, and the windowpanes rattle in a high wind. But I love being here with Mother and Father and Betsy and the little ones. Even Michael sometimes, when he comes home for the weekend. It's very funny to think of my big brother as a university student. 'We're growing up, little sister,' he says to me, although I don't feel grown-up in the slightest. Do you? I hardly recognise myself in the looking glass, with my hair up and my skirts down. I still feel like a little girl inside.

Working life is good. The orphanage is a wonderful institution. We take little children who would otherwise be sent to the workhouse or end up starving on the streets. It really is so sad – there are far more children than we can ever help. We get so many women in trouble coming to the doors, begging for our help. And most of them we have to send away. Sometimes it is women who are not married and have no way of supporting an infant. And sometimes they simply cannot feed or house another child. Miss Jessop says very often the babies we cannot take are abandoned in the street or given to baby farmers to raise, and many of them die.

The youngest children go out to foster families in the local area. They come back to us at five, which is when they start in my school. I am teaching the smallest children, and the little ones are so sweet. They are always wanting to climb onto my lap and put their arms around me. I wish I could take them all home! They leave us at fourteen, the girls mostly to domestic service, the boys to the navy.

Your industrious friend,

Polly

P.S. Do you think your grandmother would let you come and visit us, Tirzah? Could you come for Christmas again? You know we would love to have you. Mother still talks about that Christmas when you dressed up as Judith for the charades and chopped off Michael's head into the basket.

45 Park Lane
Liverpool
27th November 1896

Dear Sophia,

I know Tirzah said to write one letter to you both at once, and I have (I sent it to Tirzah, who I suppose will pass it on to you), but I felt I must add a few short lines just to you, Sophia. Do you think her grandmother really is as awful as she says, or is it just Tirzah being Tirzah? I showed Mother her letter, and she said that some women do very well as housekeepers for their relations, but Tirzah is a girl who needs a bit of a life of her own. I think she's right. I can't imagine what her parents are thinking letting her stay with that awful woman. Couldn't she go out to India with them?

I hope your aunt and cousins aren't too hideous, and the men are perfectly charming,

Polly

Bannon House
Abyford
Perthshire
30th November 1896

Dear Polly and Sophia,

Oh, Lord! What wouldn't I give to be in your house again, Polly? Would your mother like a nursery governess for the little ones? I could feed them bread and milk and tell them stories and teach them to write. She wouldn't even have to pay me – just let me wear your cast-off dresses and go to dances with you. *Do* you go to dances? You didn't say. You cannot work every hour in an orphanage.

I asked my grandmother about coming to stay with you. I planned it all very carefully. I reminded her of those Christmases I spent with you – how respectable your father is (she likes doctors; our local doctor is practically the only person who ever visits – she is a fearful hypochondriac). I asked him if he thought she was seriously ill (I know it is very wicked of me, but I cannot help thinking that I shall only escape this prison when she dies). He laughed – hateful man! – and said, 'Don't worry, Miss Lewis, your grandmother is in excellent health. She might well live to be eighty!' Eighty! I shall be an old lady myself by then.

Anyway, I was so careful. I talked about your job in the orphanage and how virtuous you are. But to no avail. She pursed her lips at me and said, 'Great heavens, girl! Do you forget your duties? You have had your fun at school; now you must settle down and work for your living.'

She had a paid companion before me, after Aunt Lucy died, a woman called Miss Hamilton. I don't know what's happened to her now I'm here. I suppose Grandmother dismissed her. I wonder where she went? Do you think she's in the workhouse?

I would rather live in a workhouse than here. At least there would be people to talk to in a workhouse. Grandmother does not so much make conversation as *lecture*. 'Sit up, Tirzah!' 'Stop making that ghastly face, Tirzah!' 'Stop *sulking*!'

She wants the sort of granddaughter who just sits there and does as she's told. Well, that's not me. I don't want to just sit. I want to do things.

'Can I take the omnibus into town? I need a new trim for my hat.'

'Can I call on the vicar?' It is not the vicar I am interested in calling on, of course, but his curate, who is twenty-two. He looks deathly dull – pale, with straggly sideburns and a horrible Adam's apple, which bobs about when he swallows. But he is at least young. I would rather marry a curate than live with Grandmother for the rest of her life.

'Is there *no one* under forty in this village, Grandmother?' There isn't, I don't think, apart from the curate. Not anyone Grandmother would let me talk to. There are some younger girls in the cottages, but they just stare as I walk past, and giggle. I wonder if I could pretend to be doing philanthropy – taking them soup or whatever. Do people actually do that outside of novels? But would anyone want to talk to an awful prig who brought them soup?

There are young men in the cottages too. I can see them drinking outside the Durham Ox on Saturday afternoons. They are not at all the sort of men Grandmother would approve of – they are working men, labourers – but goodness, they are so . . . so alive and *male*. NOT like the curate. Perhaps I shall run away with a blacksmith. It would be better than spending the next twenty years of my life fetching handkerchiefs for Grandmother.

Do you really like working in an orphanage, Polly? You sound as if you do. I wish there was something I loved like that. Do you remember how I was going to be a singer at school? It all seemed so easy back then. But I wouldn't have the first idea how one even goes about becoming one. I suppose you can't really walk up to the Royal Opera House with your music and ask to speak to the director, like you can in *Girl's Own* stories.

I remember when I talked to Mr Wallasey about it at school. He was very gentle and sweet, and said that while people do earn a living singing at concerts, they are generally professionally trained, in conservatoires and things. And you need a lot more than half an hour of singing lessons a week from the man who arranges the music for the church choir. I expect he was really telling me I would never be good enough, in the nicest possible way. Do they have singers at any of your balls, Sophia? Have you met any aristocracy? Is anyone in love with you yet? How many balls do you go to, and what do you wear, and what do you eat, and is there champagne, and how late is it that you come home?

I have never been so bored in all my life. Write back quickly before I expire.

Your friend,

Tirzah

12 Wimpole Street
London
2nd December 1896

Dear Polly and Tirzah,

What a lot of questions, Tirzah! My life is very busy. We go to balls three or four times a week. They start at ten and finish at four or five in the morning, sometimes later. We usually stay until the end, although my aunt is nodding in her chair by one. We come home by carriage and tumble into bed. We often do not wake until nearly noon. It is very decadent, and I wonder if Mummy and Daddy know what we are doing. I do not tell them, of course.

There's usually a buffet, and supper, and honestly the food is rather wonderful. Lobster, and little cakes, and ices and all sorts. Yes, there is champagne, and wine, though Aunt Eliza does not permit us girls to drink much. She said we must keep our wits about us if we are to catch husbands. We drink a little, though, just to show we are not prigs. It is all very careful. (I don't know if the real aristocracy behave like this or if it is just Aunt Eliza. She is so anxious that I will say or do something wrong. She insists on telling everyone that I am her poor niece from the country, who has not been much in society. I don't know what society we girls are supposed to have been in – we are all just out of the schoolroom or finishing school. My cousins went to finishing school in Paris, of course. Lucky beasts. Imagine, Paris!)

There are singers sometimes, and bands. I don't know how one would get a job as a singer, though, and it doesn't look a bit respectable. Some of them sing in nightclubs too! Uncle Simon told me. Your grandmother would be horrified if you tried singing with men in nightclubs, in the sort of dresses those women wear. And honestly, Tirzah, I'm not sure you would be very safe. I know I'm sounding awfully middle-aged, but I think you might be better off at home.

It is unfair, isn't it? If we were men, there wouldn't be any of this bother about marrying well. We could go off to university and become lawyers or clergymen or go into business. You could run away and join the army – you'd like that. But what are my choices if I do not find a husband? Staying at home with Mummy and Daddy. Teaching. Being a governess or a companion. Or a nurse. That's about it, honestly. And there's nothing wrong with any of those things – I'm so glad you like teaching, Polly. But somehow at school we seemed to have more options. We were always learning about Florence Nightingale, or the Brontë sisters, or Queen Victoria. It seemed quite likely that we would all grow up to be great women, probably without having to try very hard.

Real life, it turns out, isn't like that at all.

Remember how I wanted to be a journalist when I was at school? A girl reporter like Nellie Bly. It seemed so easy then. I did actually ask one of Daddy's friends about it, just in case the Season didn't work. He sucked his teeth and said maybe the knitting page or the problem page, unless I wanted to write for a women's publication. He sounded so sneery when he said it, I didn't want to pursue it somehow.

Anyway. Enough of school. Yes, of course I've met aristocrats. So many, it's getting rather boring. No, I am not in love, and I do not think I shall be.

There is one man who's interested in me, though. His name is Lord St John, and he is very old – about thirty-five, I think! He is not handsome, but he has a kind face. I think kindness is very important.

He's the youngest son, and he has three older brothers. But he's currently running the estate – two of his older brothers are in the army and the church, and the eldest lives in London and isn't interested in the country at all. But St John likes looking after the land. He keeps talking to me about horses and cows and prize pigs. I confess, I am not very interested in prize pigs! He is rather dull company. And he treads on my toes. But Aunt Eliza says he has come to London to find a wife, and he is more interested in me than in any other lady. So.

If I could get married to a man with money, my sisters could do the Season with me next year, and they would not have the shame of being the poor relation. And if I do not marry, I shall be exiled back home to live with Mummy and Daddy. This is my one chance to make a good match, and I shan't throw it away.

I miss you all so much. Take care of yourselves. Tirzah, please don't do anything stupid.

Your socialite friend,

Sophia

P.S. Dear Polly, I know Tirzah likes to exaggerate, but it can't be very jolly for her, locked up in a dull house with an old woman and no fun. I think your mother is right. I wish I could invite her here – her grandmother might agree to Mayfair if not Liverpool – but since I'm only here on sufferance myself, I can't invite guests of my own. Maybe her grandmother will tire of having her around. She can't be much earthly good as a companion. I know I joke about my aunt and cousins, but it is hard work being everybody's runaround, and you need much good humour and self-assurance. I'm sure Tirzah spends her days sighing and complaining. Perhaps her grandmother will see sense eventually and . . . Well, I don't know what. Let her come to one of us for the holidays, at least. And then perhaps she could find herself a husband. If you are young and lively and not so picky about who you settle down with, it's very easy to end up with *somebody*. There are plenty of old men who aren't so choosy. They seem to think a poor relation is easy pickings.

P.P.S. Her parents aren't in India. They died of cholera when she was a baby. She told me so in confidence ages ago.

Best love – Sophia

45 Park Lane
Liverpool
5th December 1896

Dear Tirzah and Sophia,

I suppose I should be pleased about your lord, Sophia – goodness, you, married to a lord! It sounds like something out of a fairytale. But do you really want to be married to someone you don't love? Marriage is for the rest of your life. I know you feel like you ought to help your sisters, but really, is it worth spending your whole life with a bore for? It doesn't seem like it to me.

As for being sent home and never getting another chance at the Season – well, as someone who is living at home and has never even been to London, let alone *met* a member of the aristocracy, I don't think that's such a disaster. There is life in the provinces, you know! I'm a member of a tennis club, and I play bridge on Fridays, and Mother and I are going to a course of lectures in the city hall. They're frightfully interesting. Well, they vary. There was one on science, with a fellow who blew up lots of things – that was fun. The last experiment he said, 'You really have to be jolly careful with this one,' and then blew his eyebrows off! And last week there was a lady talking about Millicent Fawcett and what a good idea it would be if women got the vote. Mother and I both thought she was ever so sensible and convincing.

There are dances too. Michael and Betsy and I went to one last Saturday. There was a big navy boat in the docks, and they put on a dance for the sailors. It is a good way to meet young men, as of course there are none working in the orphanage. We are a mostly female lot! I like it – it reminds me of school, a bit. Although of course there are boy orphans here. More boys than girls, if truth be told. It's much easier to persuade adopters to take on little girls. More fool them! The girls are just as rough as the boys when they want to be. And they are more bothered about being adopted, somehow. The boys just want someone to love them, but the girls notice that they're different to their parents, and they worry about it. We get more girls coming back to us than we do boys.

The only man you might possibly call eligible is Mr Thompson, who is the superintendent. Superintendents of orphanages are supposed to be penny-pinching villains, like Mr Bumble in *Oliver Twist*. But Mr Thompson is not a villain. He's nice and rather worn around the edges, like old leather, or a letter from an old friend that's lived in the bottom of your pocket for too long. He interviewed me when I came to work here and said, 'We're very glad to have you, Miss Anniston, and we hope you shall stay with us a good long time.' Wasn't that a nice thing to say? He cares about the children too;

you can see that. He lives in poky little rooms next to the refectory, and Miss Martin, who teaches the older infants, told me it was because he gave up his official apartments to make space for a proper playroom for the little ones and a sewing room for the big girls.

There is something the matter with him – I'm not sure what, exactly, but he walks with crutches, and his legs are all twisted, and he often looks tired and drawn. I think he's in quite a lot of pain, though he doesn't say so. It's funny, though. I had thought the children might laugh at him – you know what children are like – but they don't, at all. They treat him with the utmost seriousness and respect, listening quietly when he talks to them, which I can assure you doesn't always happen! The only time I ever saw a child say anything awful about him was a little boy who had just come to the home from a terribly rough family. He was doing an imitation of Mr Thompson, pretending to walk like he does. And these two older boys, very calmly, just went up to him and said, 'We don't do that here.' That was all. But he stopped – and I never saw him do it again.

Miss Jessop (she's the school headmistress – a very important person) told me that the superintendent they had before him kept the children on a starvation diet on principle, the way they do in workhouses. He said parents shouldn't expect charities to care for their children if they were reckless enough not to provide for them themselves. I don't know what happened to the money he didn't spend on food, but I can guess.

Anyway, so then there was a cholera epidemic, and a lot of children died, and the trustees got suspicious and gave him the boot and appointed Mr Thompson instead. A jolly good thing too.

The children are such dears. I can't understand how anyone could ever want to hurt them. You try not to have favourites, but you do, of course. There is a little boy in my class who I wish I could adopt. His name is Nicholas, and he is just five. He is ever so sweet and earnest. You can tell which children came from loving families and which were neglected and knocked about, and I would stake my life that somebody somewhere once loved Nicholas very much. I wonder what happened to them?

I am sorry this letter has ended so gloomily. I do not mean it to be. I do honestly love my job, but it *does* break my heart sometimes.

Yours,

Polly

P.S. I quite agree about the situations available for women. It is not much better for the working classes. Most of our girls go into service, you know – that or the mills and the factories. No matter how hard your life is, Tirzah, it would be worse living in a freezing attic somewhere, getting up at six a.m. to light the fires.

Do you know, there's a village near Oxford where the entire female population work as washerwomen for the students? Imagine a future where they could all go and be poets and scientists and politicians instead!

45 Park Lane
Liverpool
5th December 1896

Dear Sophia,

How funny about Tirzah's parents – she told me they were in India. She said her father was a colonel in the army and her mother was a socialite who danced at three different balls every week. She told *me* in confidence too, and said I wasn't to tell anyone because her grandmother thought dancing was immoral. It sounds absurd written down like that, but I believed it absolutely when I was eleven.

I wonder what the truth is. I wonder if Tirzah even knows. Do you think maybe she's the secret love child of her aunt Lucy, and that's why she was never allowed home in the holidays?

Have you ever met her grandmother? You've known Tirzah longer than I have – I was eleven when I came to school, but you were nine. And Tirzah had been there since she was seven, hadn't she?

Best love – Polly

Bannon House
Abyford
Perthshire
The Depths of Despair
Hell
8th December 1896

Dear girls,

I have been investigating all the male options in Grandmother's village. There are not many.

There is the curate. And if one married him, one would have to be a vicar's wife and spend all day being polite to old women at church. I cannot quite see it. Also, I don't think he likes me. He always looks appalled when I come too close, and he never knows quite what to say to me. So I do not think I will be marrying him, somehow.

There is Garth, the blacksmith's son. I like Garth. He is twenty-one and built like a horse, with a broad neck and real muscles. When I go into the village to buy toffees, I like to stop on the way back and watch him work. His arms and his neck are always covered in sweat from the furnace.

Garth is a flirt. He flirts with all the village girls, and with me. I think I could do anything sinful I wanted with Garth, and he wouldn't care. He probably does sinful things every Saturday after he finishes work. Plenty of the village girls would be sinful with him if he was willing.

I would rather not die a virgin if I can avoid it.

That's it, anyway. That's the whole unmarried male population of the entire village, unless I want to marry Old Joe, who is eighty-seven, or the butcher's boy, who is fourteen and has a horrible crush on me. He is an actual child, though. His voice hasn't broken yet. And really, I do have *some* self-respect. It's disappearing rapidly, though, the longer I stay here.

If I had the first idea how one got a job singing in a nightclub, I would run away tomorrow.

Yours, lusting after young men with muscular forearms,

Tirzah

Wimpole Street
London
10th December 1896

TIRZAH,

For God's sake, Tirzah, DO NOT do anything so stupid. I cannot tell from your letter if you are joking or not, but I am deadly serious. What if you were to have a child? Your grandmother would probably send you off to a nunnery. And worse, what if the local society got to hear of it? You would have *no* chance of ever marrying anyone. Just imagine how bad it would be for you if he boasted of this in the alehouses.

You will not die a virgin. I cannot imagine a world in which that would be possible. Polly and I will try to plan something for you, but please, this isn't the way out, please, darling. Do think better of it.

Sophia

The Slough of Despond
12th December 1896

Dear Sophia,

Do not worry. I'm not serious. Probably. Although I do wish *something* would happen. Sometimes at dinner I look at the table, all laid out with the best china, and wonder what they would do if I yanked the cloth off the tabletop and sent everything crashing to the floor. One day I'll be so miserable, I'll actually do it.

I've started thinking of new ways to annoy my grandmother. When I read to her, I change the story and see how long it is before she notices. I put in a whole speech about the cruelty of keeping young girls at home in the last novel I read to her. She did not suspect a thing. But then I made the mistake of putting an attractive young blacksmith into one of the Waverley novels, which unfortunately she knows too well to be fooled by.

'WHAT did you say, young lady?' she cried. 'Give me that book!' The game was up. And wasn't she waxy? We're now working our way through the complete works of Scott, and she keeps glaring at me if I mention anything she doesn't remember.

I also make a point to get everything wrong. If she asks me to bring her pink gloves, I bring the green ones. If she asks for her handkerchief, I bring her smelling salts. If she asks me to pick up comfits from the village, I bring peppermints. I'm hoping she will realise what a hopeless companion I am and give up. So far she mostly just flies into rages. She hasn't punished me yet, but even that would at least be interesting. I wonder what she would do. Hit me? Lock me in the attic? Probably just take my allowance away, knowing her.

There is absolutely nothing to do here except be a drudge for Grandmother, go for walks, read books, and write you letters. Oh, and sew. I do all the plain stitching and mending, as Grandmother's arthritis is so bad. It is very dull. There is a screen I am supposed to be embroidering too, but you know how I hate embroidery. It never gets any closer to being finished. Sometimes I get to go into town to spend my dress allowance. The most exciting thing that happens is church on Sundays. I even asked Grandmother if I could find someone to continue my singing lessons, but she refused. Though she does like to hear me sing in the evenings sometimes. It is not the same without accompaniment, though.

Your desperate friend,

Tirzah

Lady Hortense's ball was attended by two hundred young people. The dashing young Sebastian Fowler was much in evidence and caused a stir by dancing eight dances with Miss Sophia Fanshaw. Is love in the air for the young couple, pictured here heading for the supper table? Let's hope so!

The Illustrated London News, 12th December 1896

45 Park Lane
Liverpool
12th December 1896

Sophia! Did you see this? You, in *The Illustrated London News*! Mother's friend Mrs Hinterfield brought the clipping around to show us – she was ever so excited because she met you when you came to stay at Easter. And who is the dashing Sebastian Fowler with whom you danced eight dances? Tell us everything! We demand to know!

Polly

Wimpole Street
London
14th December 1896

Dear girls,

Oh, Sebastian Fowler! Now, *there's* a tale.

No, there isn't. He is an excessively charming and excessively aggravating young man who does not have a penny to his name. He is the third of seven children. His father, it is true, is the youngest son of an earl, but the family live all tumbled up together in a flat in Bloomsbury, of all places. I don't know how they make ends meet, for none of them seem to work and they are always complaining of being in debt; they seem to get by on charm and sheer nerve.

I cannot possibly marry him, so do not get excited. We would be perpetually poor, and it would be an utter disaster. Mummy has already written to tell me so, and so has Grandmother. Aunt Eliza said, rather laconically, 'Really, darling, it wouldn't be wise at all.' Cousin Mariah, far more spitefully, 'You needn't think Sebastian is doing anything but toying with you, Sophia, so don't put on airs. He hasn't a penny to call his own, and if he's going to marry anyone, it ought to be an heiress.' She is just jealous, because Sebastian *is* handsome (I can tell you that without sounding stuck-up, can't I?), and it is her third Season and no one is so much as looking.

Anyway, I have told Sebastian all this, but he will keep bothering me. He is a devilishly good dancer, and he does make me laugh, which so few men do. He threatened to take me home and introduce me to all his brothers and sisters, which I must say sounded more fun than the usual staid tea parties and supper parties I get invited to. His eldest brother, Dorian, is a terrible gambler and a great worry to them all, and his sister Helena is a socialist and a suffragist who spends all her time going on marches and selling copies of socialist newspapers in the streets – imagine! He has a little sister called Athena – Athena! – who wants to be an actress and spends all day dressed up in bedsheets reciting Greek drama, and a little brother called Tobias who likes animals and fills the flat with goldfish and stag beetles and toads and suchlike. Doesn't it all sound fun? Sebastian says it's rather less fun when you're in the middle of it, and the flat is always noisy and chaotic, and the servants are always giving notice, and nobody can ever find any blotting paper or clean collars. I hope he does invite me round for tea, and I shall certainly go if I am invited, but it is nothing but a flirtation, do not worry. Sebastian is a great flirt and everyone's darling. It will do my stock no harm to be associated with him.

Yours practically,
Sophia

P.S. Mariah and Isabelle are sick with envy that I am in *The Illustrated London News* and they are not. They say it's only because I am hanging off the arm of a known womaniser. I simply smile and say 'Naturally!' which makes them even sicker. Ha!

Wimpole Street
London
14th December 1896

Dear Polly,

I never met Tirzah's grandmother, not once the whole time she was at school. And I never met her mother or father either. What on earth do you think the real story is?

Sophia

7 Larch End
Glasgow
14th December 1896

Dear Mother,

I am writing to you because I am in need of money. The rent is three weeks overdue, and the landlord says that if I do not pay, I will be evicted again. Please send anything you can spare to the above address, by return of post, or it will be too late.

I remain, your daughter,
Clare

Bannon House
Abyford
Perthshire
15th December 1896

Dear Mamma,

You must think it queer, me writing to you out of the blue like this. I know I never did before. The truth is, I didn't know your address. School didn't know – I did ask once, but the only address they had was Grandmother's. And Grandmother wouldn't tell me, of course. But I found a letter from you. Grandmother had thrown it straight into the wastepaper basket – only I knocked the basket over, and all the papers inside it fell out onto the floor. I started tidying them up, and that's when I found your letter.

And your address.

Mamma, it's over ten years since we saw each other. Perhaps you don't want to hear from me. But if you do, you should know that I am well.

I left school this summer, and now I am back living with Grandmother. She expects me to keep house and to be her companion, and she will not think of allowing me to marry or go anywhere or see anyone. Was she like that when you were a child and lived with her? Is that why you no longer see her? Except you do write to her.

I didn't know that. Did you write to me as well? I never received any letters, but perhaps Grandmother threw them into the fire. It's exactly the sort of thing she would do. Did you think I didn't want to write to you? Mamma, of course I did. If I'd ever got any of your letters, I would have replied at once.

I've missed you so much. I used to watch all the other girls with their mothers and wonder where you were and if you were all right and if you were even still alive. I can't tell you what a shock it gave me, seeing your name on that letter.

Mamma, how are you? Your letter sounded like you were in financial trouble. I wish I could help, but the allowance Grandmother gives me is barely enough to keep myself in hats. Are you married? You just signed the letter 'Clare', so I do not know. Do you have other children?

Please write back to me,

Tirzah

P.S. It is safe to write to me here – I get lots of letters from school friends, and Grandmother never opens them. Only perhaps it would be best to write the address in capitals, so she does not recognise your handwriting.

P.P.S. You will write back, won't you?

45 Park Lane
Liverpool
17th December 1896

Dear Sophia and Tirzah,

Oh, Sophia, Sebastian sounds absolutely wonderful. Of course I see why you can't marry him, but I do hope you get to keep him as a friend at least.

Nothing nearly as exciting as your news, but yesterday I took tea with a young gentleman too! No, not really, only Mr Thompson. He has tea with a different member of the staff every Wednesday afternoon, and today it was my turn. On Thursdays he has tea with five of the orphans. Isn't that a dear idea? He explained that it was partly to give them a treat and to break the monotony of orphanage life, and partly so they can tell him if something isn't right. They would tell him too! They have no fear of authority, and they love to complain. But Mr Thompson seems pretty able to tell the mischief-makers from the real complainants. Miss Martin told me he sacked the last teacher because she used to cane the children when they were naughty. The children told him at tea, and showed him the marks on their hands, and she was gone. My little brothers are all caned at school, but Mr Thompson won't have it in his orphanage. He says they suffered enough before they came here, and it does no good to frighten them.

I was a little nervous about my tea, but I needn't have worried. He was very kind, and he seemed really interested in all I was doing with the little ones. I told him how worried I am about Mabel Jackson's cough, and he said he would ask the doctor to look at it next time he was here. I think the doctor should look at him too; he looked tired to death. I asked him if he was all right – which was forward of me, I know, but Mother always fusses over anybody who comes to tea, so it seemed quite natural. He looked a bit surprised but said yes, he had just stayed up late looking over the accounts. He wants to apprentice some of the older boys out to tradesmen in the city, but of course that costs money, and he couldn't quite work out how to squeeze it.

I have found out more about my little Nicholas too. Today, when I was minding the little ones in their playroom, I noticed two older boys playing with him. I went over to see who they were, and it turns out they are his brothers, Robert and Daragh. They are two very earnest little chaps, aged seven and nine. Daragh has round spectacles and looks like the sort of genius child you get in boys' school stories who knows all about science. They see themselves very much as a family, despite their being in different classes, and don't mind coming to the babies' playroom to see their little brother. Nicholas obviously adores them.

I talked to them a bit and found out something of their history. Their mother is dead, and their father was a soldier. They didn't seem too sure what had happened to him – Robert thought he was dead, but Daragh insisted he was still alive and in India.

'He's going to come back and get us,' he said.

I didn't like to disabuse him of the notion. And who knows? Perhaps he's right. We have quite a lot of motherless children here whose fathers come and visit when they can. It isn't always possible for men to find someone to care for the children.

'Does he write to you?' I asked, but they shook their heads.

'That lady didn't tell him we were here,' said Daragh. 'But when he comes home, he'll see, and she'll be sorry!'

I presumed he meant whoever had brought them to the orphanage when it was found out that their mother had died.

'I'm sure she was just trying to help you,' I said.

Absolute outrage! Horror! They were practically falling over themselves to tell me about it.

It turns out 'she' is not a district visitor or a poor-law guardian, but their stepmother! Their father married her before he went to India, to make sure there was someone to look after the boys, but after he'd gone, she put them in the orphanage!

I almost don't want to investigate any further, because probably there will be some very mundane and ordinary explanation – perhaps the father is dead, and the stepmother cannot afford to keep them on her own. Or perhaps she got ill, or was deemed an unfit guardian. I am sure the truth will be much less dramatic than the boys' version of it – that she abandoned them and is living in luxury on the money the boys' father sends home for their keep. But I must admit, I'm worried.

What if they're right?

Yours anxiously,

Polly

P.S. Tirzah, are you sure you can't come here for Christmas? Mother asked me to check. I know you said you couldn't, but . . . do try. It won't feel like Christmas without you.

Bannon House
Abyford
Perthshire
18th December 1896

Dear Sophia and Polly,

Goodness, your lives are thrilling! Why, oh why do you get to be you while I'm stuck being boring old me?

Polly, of course you should investigate! If it's nothing, it won't matter. But what if it's true?

Sophia, I think Sebastian sounds wonderful. I think you should marry him and damn the consequences. Why does it have to be you who all your sisters rely on? Why can't it be Louisa or Becky or one of the others? I must say, it makes me sick to think of you being introduced to all these glamorous men, and throwing it all away to marry some rich dullard.

I *wish* I could come to yours for Christmas, Polly. But no chance. My grandmother has no intention of spending Christmas alone, so I will be here, bored to absolute death, just me and her all day. I can't bear it.

Sophia, what are you doing for Christmas? You never said. Are you spending it with the relations or what? I know you think yourself very sensible and practical, but I think you're a fool.

Yours, forthright, right, and right miserable,

Tirzah

Wimpole Street
London
20th December 1896

Dear Polly and Tirzah,

Well, I'm not going to marry Sebastian. I would be a selfish pig if I did so, after all the money Mummy's spent on getting me here and kitting me out. And if Mariah and Isabelle find husbands this year, Aunt Eliza won't even be doing another Season, so it's the only chance any of us will get.

Polly, of course you must try to find out more, but please do be careful. These are real children, not characters in a penny dreadful. Don't get their hopes up.

I'm sorry. I'm in a foul mood today. I'll tell you why – I can't tell anyone else – and then maybe you'll understand.

I had my first proposal.

It was from George Carroll. Have I told you about George? A perfectly respectable young man, not too wealthy but not too shabby either (he's another youngest son). Rather shy and awkward, with a habit of laughing a little too much when he doesn't know what to say. He's going into the clergy.

I was rather worried he was going to ask me – he'd been getting that look men *do* get, and I'm sure it was because I was kind to him and didn't laugh at him the way some of the other girls do. Perhaps that was wrong? It is so hard to know the difference between being kind and polite and breaking a boy's heart.

Anyway. All this evening he kept hinting that he was going to ask me something, and I had a horrible feeling I knew what it was, but of course I couldn't say anything in case I was wrong. We were down to dance the waltz, but he begged me to step outside with him as he had something very important to tell me, and then – oh!

I shall not go into details. But although he was very polite and understanding, it was *so awful*. I felt terrible for him; he was so flustered and embarrassed, I am sure I am the first girl he has ever managed to ask. He must feel so horrible! But also, I *could not* marry him. Even if he had all the riches in Arabia, I could not. I knew he could not make me happy, and though I think I should do a reasonable job of making him happy, there is a line – there must be! – and he, poor boy, was on the wrong side of it.

Oh, goodness. Maybe I have made a terrible mistake. Perhaps I am not cut out for marrying for money after all.

I'm sorry, girls. I shall be more cheerful next time. I must run, as I am catching the train this afternoon. I am going home for Christmas, for two lovely, lovely weeks! Hurrah, hurrah, hurrah!

Your foolish friend,

Sophia

45 Park Lane
Liverpool
21st December 1896

Dear Sophia and Tirzah,

Oh, Sophia, I am sorry. I am, really. I would so hate to have to turn anyone down. It was bad enough telling Michael's friend Davy that I didn't want him to be my beau, and that was when we were twelve! Turning down a marriage proposal is much worse.

In a way, it's good, though, that someone has asked. It means you must be doing something right. Surely?

Much excitement here, as today was the last day of school before the holidays. I will be sorry to miss all the Christmas celebrations but selfishly glad to get a break – the lot of a teacher is a tiring one!

Christmas at the orphanage does sound fun, though. Under the previous superintendent, it was rather a sorry affair – the children got an orange each and a roast dinner cooked by a local church. This year there is to be a trip to the pantomime – imagine! Mr Thompson spoke to the theatre, and they donated the tickets as a goodwill gesture. There will be an article about it in the *Liverpool Echo*, of course, but it was still jolly generous of them. There will be new toys for the playrooms – donations from local businesses – and a new book for each of the children. We teachers have been cutting them all open, ready to present them on Christmas morning. I am a little sorry about this – there is something so wonderful about a new book with uncut pages – but I must admit that letting our orphans loose with paper knives might be unwise.

Toys are a continual problem in the orphanage. Lots of our children still have family – either parents who can't look after them, or aunts and uncles and grandparents. So toys do find their way in. The old superintendent banned them, which was the cause of many tears. Mr Thompson allows them, but of course they are always getting lost or stolen, and there is nowhere to keep them.

Mr Thompson says that it is important to remember that the children are people, and that being a person in an institution is hard. Another thing he's done is insist all the children have their own uniforms with their own names in them, and that they get back their own clothes from the wash. This is a very unpopular innovation with the staff, as it makes laundry day much more complicated, and of course the children are always getting their clothes mixed up. In the old days, there were sets of uniforms in small, medium, and large, and you got whichever set was on top of the pile. But Mr Thompson says nobody wants to be dressed in another child's clothes, and having their own uniform will encourage them to keep it nice. When I talk to the children, they all say they prefer it this way, especially the girls. And even the staff admit that the children look better in clothes that are the right size.

Wasn't that a clever thought? I would never, ever have thought of that. I asked him how he knew how the children felt, and he said, 'I was in a sanatorium for two years when I was a child. I know a lot about institutions.'

I do love my job! I wouldn't give up going to work for a million pounds.

Much love and a merry Christmas to one and all!

Polly

Flat 4, Marsh Mansions
Haydown Street
Bloomsbury
London
21st December 1896

Dear Miss Fanshaw,

I hope you can forgive me the impertinence of writing to you like this (and of asking your cousin Mariah for your Derbyshire address). If we are to have any sort of friendship (and I do hope we can be friends – don't you?), you'll have to forgive a great many impertinences, I'm afraid. I mean no harm by them. Do please inform me at once if I have offended, and I will pluck out my eye, my pen, my inkwell, and my writing hand (I must save the other for the plucking) and deliver them to your doorstep tied up with a bow. I may need someone else to tie the bow, but I hope you'd be understanding in the circumstances.

I merely wanted to tell you how beautiful you looked in your blue dress at Mrs Walker's tea party, how refreshing it was to see a young lady so willing to laugh at herself, how kind you were to your aunt and cousins, and how I burned with rage to see how they leaned on you. I am going to miss you like the devil when you're away – for two whole weeks, damn you! Also, I woke up this morning with a terrible thought: had I made life difficult for you by leaping in like I did and offering to fetch your aunt's wrap and pour her tea for her? Did she take it as an insult? Are you allowed followers? I do not mean to make your life harder, though I cannot contain my fury that an angel such as yourself should be forced to act as an unpaid servant.

Please reassure me that your aunt has not repaid my kindness by forcing you to sleep in the cellar with the rats and the black beetles, and I shall remain,

your obedient servant,

Sebastian Fowler

Willow House
Little Glebeford
Derbyshire
23rd December 1896

Dear Mr Fowler,

Thank you for your letter of the 21st. It does not offend, though if you are to send me anything tied up with a bow, body parts would not be my preference. Your deference does you credit, however, as does your kindness to me at Mrs Walker's tea party.

Please be assured that my aunt is not cruel, and she was rather touched, if anything, by your kindness towards her. However, I take issue with your insinuation that I am an 'unpaid servant'. I am nothing of the kind. My aunt has sponsored my Season, at great expense to herself, and if in return I must fetch her book and find her spectacles and answer her letters, I consider it an extremely reasonable exchange.

The tone of your letter seemed to imply that an 'angel' such as myself should not be working at all, which I dispute. Gabriel himself served as messenger to the Lord on several occasions, and while I own that delivering glad tidings to Mary and Joseph is rather a more glamorous occupation than RSVPing to party invitations, the principle remains. Gentlemen work – my father is a painter – why should not gentlewomen? And what, when it comes down to it, is so demeaning about being a servant anyway? If I do not find a husband by the summer, I shall no doubt be working as a governess or a companion, and I will not consider it below my dignity to do so.

If, in the light of this information, you would prefer to cease this correspondence, I will understand.

I remain your (and Aunt Eliza's) obedient servant,

Sophia Fanshaw

7 Larch End
Glasgow
23rd December 1896

Dear Miss Lewis,

I am returning the enclosed letter. Miss Clare Lewis no longer lives here. I regret to inform you that she was behind on the rent, and it was necessary to ask her to vacate the property. If you could see your way fit to paying the £4, 7s, 6d owing, I would be extremely obliged.

Your obedient servant,
Vera Blake (Mrs)

Flat 4, Marsh Mansions
Haydown Street
Bloomsbury
London
26th December 1896

My dear Miss Fanshaw,

Cease this correspondence? My dearest Gabriel! I am, if anything, more in awe of you than I ever was before. You are of course entirely right – hard work is a noble business (or so I'm told; I am, I'm afraid, the laziest soul in Christendom). Your willingness to answer correspondence for your supper is further proof of your superiority of soul.

Just look at you! Beautiful, clever, witty AND noble. What is a poor young man to do? For it is now my turn to abase myself before you. Do not think I am unaware of what you are doing. You wish – from the kindness and honesty which are so essential to your being – to show how unsuitable our match would be. You are, I own, a very poor fish from a purely mercenary perspective. But consider yourself in comparison to your fisherman! Just look at me!

1. I am incredibly lazy. I have never done a day's paid work in my life, never gained a university degree, never even finished my prep most days at school.

2. I am penniless. Penniless, of course, in the peculiarly upper-class sense that involves several servants, an excellent, well-proportioned flat in Bloomsbury, and attendance at most of the parties of the Season.
3. I, too, am expected to marry well, but fortunately (or unfortunately, depending on your perspective), my family is so disorganised that this obligation is only a very vague one, and if I do not fulfil it, no one will do more than sigh and hope vaguely that one of my many and varied siblings will do their duty instead. My parents married for love, so they can hardly complain if their children do the same. In my family, romance is always exalted above mere trifles like bread and butter, I am sorry to say. (As, now I think of it, is trifle. My family would eat trifle every day if it occurred to them. Perhaps this should go in the 'pro' column – what do you think of trifle for tea?) Incidentally, you said your father was a painter. He isn't Willard Fanshaw by any chance, is he? I saw an exhibition of his work a few years ago – marvellous stuff! I expect every second gentleman you dance with says this to you, but really, your father is a genius. What is it like to be the offspring of a genius? Are you one too?

4. Sorry, I digress. I should put that as fault four. A tendency to digression.
5. I am also fearfully disorganised and quite atrociously untidy. You, I am sure, are neatness and charm itself. I, alas, am not. This would likely cause conflict. Our home would never be in order.
6. Damn. I did not mean to mention our future home so early in our correspondence. I meant to come at it sideways, like a butterfly hunter, when I had won you over with my charm and wit. I am quite charming and witty, you know. At least I hope you know. If you do not find me so, I fear I must give up all hopes of our marrying, for I have very little else to offer you.

I shall not despair. I shall move onto my advantages, which fortunately are many.

1. I am a cheerful soul, not prone to depression. In this I think we are similar.
2. I am, as I have previously mentioned, extremely charming and witty. I may not own an estate in Scotland and a house in Mayfair, but I trust I shall always be able to make you laugh.
3. I am not unhandsome. In fact, I would go so far as to say that I am tolerably attractive. If one

believes the poets, many marriages have been based on less.

4. I am moderately intelligent. I always did all right in school, despite the aforementioned laziness. This could be useful?
5. I *believe* you like me. I would not dream of importuning you in this way if I thought you did not. I sincerely like you. I think we fit together well. Your practicality and my optimism. Your good sense and my wild schemes. A shared kindness, generosity of spirit, a general amusement at the follies of the world. Do you not think we could be happy together?

Oh, dear. I did not mean this letter to be a proposal of marriage, but somehow it seems to have happened despite myself. This is always happening to me. (Not proposing. Believe it or not, I have made it to the grand old age of twenty-two without ever proposing to anyone. But the one thing leading to another.) Please indicate by return of post if such a thing might be amenable to you, and I will arrange a more romantic declaration. I know a fellow with a string quartet if such a thing might appeal.

Yours foolishly,

Sebastian Fowler

P.S. I hope you had a happy Christmas. I had a perfectly jolly one, though Helena and I got rather tight at a socialist party, and Helena nearly got arrested for knocking off a policeman's hat. I think she would have got away with it if she hadn't yelled 'Capitalist scum!' at him too. But we ran away before he caught up with us.

Bannon House
Abyford
Perthshire
26th December 1896

Dear Polly and Sophia,

Well, Sophia, I know I should be sorry about you and Mr Carroll, but I'm afraid I can't be very sympathetic. If Mr Carroll is very downhearted, tell him you know a beautiful Scottish maiden who would take him off your hands without thinking twice. I don't even have to meet him. How does one apply to be a mail-order bride, do you know? I'm sure I wouldn't mind being shipped off to India to marry a colonialist. It would be better than being here.

I hope you both had nice Christmases, because I didn't. It was just Grandmother and me, and it was horribly dull. We opened the presents after breakfast. Grandmother gave me a postal order as usual. I gave her a copy of *The Time Machine*, because if I have to read another Waverley novel, I shall scream. She made a sort of 'huh' noise – almost like she thought it was funny. I didn't think she had a sense of humour. I also got presents from the servants, and from *you*, of course. Sophia, your hat is the most beautiful thing I have ever owned. Even Grandmother was impressed! However much did it cost? Or does everyone wear hats like that in London?

Afterwards we just humphed around, not knowing what to do, then we had lunch, which admittedly was nice – Grandmother is not a Scrooge. And that was it. We sat around reading our new books (*thank* you, Polly – without your book, I would have had to actually *talk* to her). Grandmother didn't read the Wells, though. She read a book of poems the vicar had given her. Can you even *imagine*?

Love to you both, you lucky dogs,

Tirzah

Willow House
Little Glebeford
Derbyshire
28th December 1896

Dear Tirzah and Polly,

I'll tell you a secret – the hats were old ones that Isabelle didn't want any more. She threw them carelessly at me and said, 'There you go – you haven't any money to buy new ones, have you?' They are perfectly lovely, but I'll be damned if I wear her castoffs. I'm so glad you like yours. I bet you look much more handsome in them than she did.

My Christmas was lovely. It was marvellous to be home again, to not be the poor relation, to not be dashing from party to party to party without five minutes to think. I have been sleeping for hours and hours and hours. And going for walks with the girls, and seeing my cousins on Daddy's side, and skating on the pond, and helping Mummy . . . It's been – well – lovely. (A good job I never did become a journalist, isn't it?)

It's rather strange to come back here, though. A bit like when I first came home after going away to school, and all the clothes in my wardrobe were too small, and the pictures on the wall suddenly looked childish. I'd been very into making things out of wool when I left, and it felt so strange to see all these woolly animals sitting there, that I'd outgrown. Like stepping back in time and finding I didn't fit in the past any more.

Love and plum pudding to you both,

Sophia

Willow House
Little Glebeford
Derbyshire
28th December 1896

Dear Mr Fowler,

Goodness, it does feel ridiculous to call you Mr Fowler when you write me letters like that. Can I call you Sebastian? Everyone else does. I suppose I shouldn't let you call me Sophia – it would only encourage you – but – it's so strange – I feel as though we're intimate friends already, though I have only known you a few weeks. I think you must feel the same. You don't write letters like that to everyone you know, do you?

Anyway. To answer your points: no, of course I will not marry you. Don't be absurd. And please don't tell lies. I'm not beautiful. I am a cheery little garden flower – a snapdragon or a foxglove, surrounded by hothouse bouquets. I look well enough but nothing more. Nor am I witty. Or wise. I have practical good sense, and I like to laugh. I will grow up to be a very ordinary sort of woman and, I hope, your good friend, but I am nothing special. I would ask you to be honest about that if you wish to continue this friendship. (Though don't you think the idea of exalted sorts of people is a funny one anyway? People are just people, aren't they? I've met a fair few exalted painters thanks to Daddy, and they're just people with bad haircuts who grumble about the Liberals and get cross when you forget to put sugar in their tea, same as everyone else.)

Yours,

Sophia

P.S. Trust you to have heard of Daddy! You're the first person in London who has – or at least who's made the connection to me. I don't talk about him much. He's a painter's painter, you know – everyone in the Art world gets very excited about him, but no one outside painting has ever heard of him. People don't generally know painters unless they've been dead for centuries and hung in the National Gallery. Are you an Art person? Or have you been checking up on me secretly and hoped to impress me by having heard of my father? I don't *think* that's true. But I don't really know you at all . . .

P.P.S. I had a very nice Christmas, thank you. But I think you and Helena are absurd to call a policeman capitalist scum, when he earns an honest living and you and she are the grandchildren of an earl.

45 Park Lane
Liverpool
30th December 1896

Dear Tirzah and Sophia,

Sophia, your hat! It's beautiful! Did Isabelle really not want it? Is that the truth or are you just saying that to make me feel better about just giving you a book like always?

I agree with Tirzah; I feel quite someone wearing it. Everyone said how ripping it was. It was quite the most glamorous present under my tree. And Tirzah, thank you so much for the comfits too. I have been lying in bed reading Sherlock Holmes stories and eating comfits and feeling like a duchess.

It is so strange to have all the children home for Christmas! I never really thought about what that must have been like for Mother and Father – I suppose I thought that was just what home was always like, busy and noisy and full of children. But of course it's not, most of the time, not when it's just Betsy and the little ones and me at home. Now everyone's back from school – and Michael from Edinburgh – the whole house has come alive. I shall be just as weepy as Mother and Father when they all go back.

Christmas has been Christmas, just the same as it always is – charades and plum puddings and games and all the rest. You've been missed, Tirzah! The little ones wanted to know why you weren't here, and even Michael asked where you were. Please do try to come and see us sometime. We all love you very much.

Your grace of the comfits,

Polly

Flat 4, Marsh Mansions
Haydown Street
Bloomsbury
London
30th December 1896

Dear Sophia,

I seem to have offended you again. I keep doing that. I tend to gabble when I'm nervous (as you may have noticed). I'm just so terrified that you'll decide this conversation cannot continue any longer, and I won't have managed to say all the things I need to say to you. Perhaps we could consider my undying devotion a settled issue and move on to talk about more interesting things.

For example: you say there is no such thing as an exalted person and therefore you're nothing special, but people are inherently special, aren't they? So are snapdragons and foxgloves. What could be more exalted than an English garden? I admit we should not divide people into the ordinary and extraordinary, but perhaps we're all extraordinary? Humanity itself, the whole whirling multitude of laughter and sacrifice and creation. You are perhaps no more divine than the crowds passing under my window each day. But you are no *less* divine either.

I don't want to pretend to be religious – I'm not – at least not the church-on-Sundays sort of religious. But I am a great believer in the numinousness of existence. There is something holy about a girl in a blue dress looking up and smiling as you come into a drawing room. Don't you think?

As to your father . . . I don't think I'm an Art person. Not a professional one, anyway. My mother loves art, though. She taught us drawing and painting as children, and she was very interested in our artistic education. I can't make art myself, but I'm an enthusiastic appreciator of it. And I did very much like the exhibition I saw. I was being straightforward about that, I promise. He deserves to be much better known than he is.

What does he think about your marrying for money?

Sebastian

Bannon House
Abyford
Perthshire
1st January 1897

Dear Polly and Sophia,

Well. I have news for the new year. Prepare yourselves.

I kissed Garth today.

Do not worry. Nobody saw. And I shall not do it again.

I was coming home from the grocer's in the village. I'd had a dreadfully dull day. Dreadful reading to Grandmother this morning. Dreadful chores – tidying her sitting room and running errands in the village. And then the dull tedium of the afternoon, while she had her rest and I was expected to entertain myself. I read my book for a bit, but it was a horrible bore, and I'd read it before. Reading a boring book for the second time is more misery than I can take.

In the end, I decided to wander into the village again, because honestly there is nothing else to do in this hellhole. It was a miserable sort of day, grey and misty, and hardly anyone was about. I went to the grocer's and bought a bag of peppermints because I just wanted something cheerful. I went to the bookseller's and looked at the books, but I didn't have enough money to buy one, and there wasn't anything there I really wanted anyway.

Honestly, if I had had the money, I'd have got on a train to Edinburgh, then another to London, and gone on the streets to pay my way to a career as a chorus girl. Anything, anything, anything at all would be better than this!

Anyway. I walked home the long way round past Garth's forge, as I always do nowadays. He was there on his own, so I stopped to say hello.

'Bitter day, isn't it?' he said, and I agreed that it was. That is the level of wit in Abyford, I'm afraid.

I was bored, and I knew home would be even more boring, so I came a bit closer.

'You must be very clever to make things out of metal like that,' I said. 'Isn't it frightfully difficult?'

Such is the level of my flirtation. He looked at me sideways, a bit pleased, and said, 'Not so hard if you know what you're doing.'

God, I was bored! I came a bit closer – not so close that it was dangerous, but close enough that I could see what he was doing.

'Goodness, you are strong!' I said.

At last he seemed to realise what I was doing. He gets a lot of girls flirting with him – there are usually a gaggle of shopgirls and tweenies around him – so he can't have been fool enough not to recognise it. As I write this I realise that perhaps he had known before but was trying to restrain himself around Mrs Lewis's granddaughter.

He gave me a sort of curious look and said, 'What are you doing, Miss Lewis?'

I got a bit nervous then.

'Me? Nothing! Just talking,' I said breezily. He is *so* strong. He is built like the Durham Ox on the pub sign. If he had wanted to – you know – have his wicked way with me, he could have, without blinking. I suddenly thought 'What *am* I doing?' It was like you were there in the forge with me, Sophia!

He came up to me then, and I flinched. I was suddenly frightened. He laughed a little at that.

'Playing with the rough stuff, aren't you?' he said.

It was like a challenge. I think he thought I would run away. But I didn't. I don't like to be thought afraid. I looked him straight in the eye and said, 'So what if I am?'

And then he kissed me.

It was the first time I've ever been kissed. (Have you been kissed, girls? You haven't said.) I didn't like it much. He was so forceful – I felt like he was taking something. ('Stole a kiss' sounds so romantic, but it didn't feel romantic. It felt like being robbed.) I was frightened. He smelled of beer and sweat and iron and tobacco and something smoky and leathery and horsey: the smell of the forge.

I pulled back. (Not while he was kissing me – it seemed rude. Afterwards.) I didn't want to upset him or make him think I didn't like it, which was maybe stupid, but it's how I felt. He was laughing at me.

'Go home,' he said.

So I did.

I felt awfully queer when I got home. I thought about 'ruined women' – I don't think I'm a ruined woman because I've been kissed, but I felt something a bit too close to that for comfort. Like I'd touched something I shouldn't have touched, and I didn't like it.

Oh, I'm not explaining this well! Anyway, I shan't do it again. And I shall walk home by the high street and not by the forge from now on. And I would like to know if you've ever been kissed, girls. It would make me feel better if you had.

Your not-yet-ruined friend,

Tirzah

P.S. Happy new year. If I am still here this time next year . . . Well, I won't be, that's all.

Willow House
Little Glebeford
Derbyshire
3rd January 1897

Dear Tirzah (and Polly),

My darling, darling Tirzah. Please do be careful. You are very precious – to me and to Polly. You know that, don't you?

I've been kissed too. Only once. At a Christmas party at my grandfather's house. My grandfather loved holding parties and dances, and this was a lovely messy one, with the children running about upstairs playing devil in the dark, the grown-ups dancing quadrilles and drinking downstairs, and all us young people jammed somewhere in the middle.

We are quite a crowd when my family are all together – my mother has five brothers and sisters, and although one never married and one is in India, the others have been procreating like billy-o.

Anyway. My cousin Margery and I got rather tight on wine we weren't supposed to be drinking and ended up dancing with some of the young medical students from the hospital where my cousin George was studying. And . . . well . . .

But I *know* I told you about this, because you both thought it was hilarious. He was a very gruff Scotsman called Angus, and he kept saying 'Are you all right? Are you sure?' which was maybe not very romantic either.

Tirzah, I think you might be asking because you want to be reassured that you didn't do anything terrible. So I think you are very foolish, and it could have ended much worse, but no, I don't think you're a bad person. I think you're our darling Tirzah whom we love very much – only, please don't do it again, will you?

Oh, dear! I'm jolly glad your grandmother doesn't read your letters, that's all.

So much love,

Sophia

45 Park Lane
Liverpool
4th January 1897

Dear Tirzah (and Sophia),

Oh, my darling girl! I wish I were there in your room so I could put my arms around you and tell you how much I love you.

Yes, I have been kissed. Twice, actually. Once by a friend of Michael's – a boy named Sam. He came to stay in the holidays for a week, and he asked me very politely if he might, and I said yes, so he did. We walked out together for a whole four days, and then he went back home, and I never heard from him again. I was fourteen. I *must* have told you about him, but perhaps I never told you about the kiss. I think maybe I was too shy. But I remember you and Sophia laughing about him and writing his name all over my slate.

The other time was my friend Joan's brother Thomas. That was last year, at Joan's birthday party. We were supposed to be having a garden party, but it rained, so we had a tea party inside, with a gramophone and dancing – all very childish, but good fun nonetheless. We ended up playing dares, and someone dared Thomas to say who he thought the prettiest girl in the room was, and he said me. Of course everyone got very excited about that, and when it was my turn, they dared me to say if I would kiss Thomas if he asked me, and I said yes. So then when it was Thomas's turn, they dared him to ask me, and . . . Well, that was that, really. It wasn't very romantic. But it was very sweet and innocent.

Tirzah, please don't walk past the forge again. I do worry about you, you know.

Sending so much love it will probably rub off on the postman (so watch out!),

Polly

P.S. Dear Sophia, I am frightfully worried about Tirzah, you know. I think she will probably end up running away with the first single man to saunter across her path. There are women who could make the best of a loveless marriage – I think you are probably one of them. But Tirzah isn't. She doesn't have the self-preservation instinct. She needs to be absolutely adored by someone very kind and sensible and forgiving.

Oh, how I hate that grandmother of hers! I would happily strangle her, and then Tirzah could come and live with us. (I am certain she doesn't have any other relations; her parents must be long gone or they would have said something before now, surely? And if they are still alive, they have played so very little part in her life, I think they can be safely ignored.)

Polly xx

Wimpole Street
London
6th January 1897

Dear Polly,

I agree. I wish I could help her, but I'm damned if I know how. Perhaps if I do manage to marry well and live in a grand mansion somewhere, her grandmother might be snobbish enough to accept a visit for Tirzah. And then I can parade lots of nice eligible bachelors in front of her. We can but hope.

Your loving friend,
Sophia xx

Flat 4, Marsh Mansions
Haydown Street
Bloomsbury
London
7th January 1897

Dear Miss Fanshaw,

I heard from Jack Cornwall that you were back in London. Would you do me the honour of coming to tea at the above address on January 11th? Your aunt too, of course. Around 2 p.m., if that's convenient.

Yours extremely properly,
Sebastian Fowler

P.S. The Aged Parents and all the offspring will be there too, I expect. I told them about you, and they're fearfully curious.

12 Wimpole Street
London
7th January 1897

Dear Mr Fowler,

Thank you so much for your invitation. (Goodness, you were proper!) My aunt and I would be delighted to attend.

Yours, extremely respectably,
Sophia Fanshaw

Bannon House
Abyford
Perthshire
8th January 1897

Dear Polly and Sophia,

I walked past Garth's forge today. I was going to go the direct way, and then I thought – hell! I live here too, don't I? So I went. I felt rather foolish, but nothing happened. Two of the barmaids from the Durham Ox were there, talking and flirting. He ignored me and I ignored him. So that's that. Thank goodness.

Your foolish friend,
Tirzah

Wimpole Street
London
11th January 1897

Dear Polly and Tirzah,

Well, I am back in London. It felt very strange to be running errands for Aunt Eliza after being the glamorous older sister at home. But I had the most delightful pick-me-up. I went round to Sebastian's house for tea! Aunt Eliza came too to chaperone, and also because she is fearfully curious about them all. Isabelle and Mariah were *not* invited, and weren't they green?

Sebastian's household were all perfectly charming, and really, it wasn't nearly so bad as he'd made out, though it *was* rather noisy and cluttered. There were books everywhere, some of them rather shocking (I made Sebastian put one away before Aunt Eliza saw it, but he thought it frightfully funny that I would care). His father is an absolute dear, and his mother rather ineffectual – she spent the whole visit sitting in a chair, fanning herself and saying 'Really, darling!' and 'Heavens!' while everyone ignored her.

There was an actual monkey, called JoJo, who belonged to the little brother, who is a darling. There was a nanny, but nobody seemed to have the least expectation that the children should stay in the nursery;

they came in and out of the drawing room and demanded cakes and performed monologues, and I know it sounds awful (Aunt Eliza was most shocked), but honestly, after all the carefully arranged socialising of the last few months, it was a joy to be somewhere so natural and artless. Though they aren't artless, of course, not really; eccentrics like that never are. It was at least half put-on – the older children, at least, and certainly Sebastian. He knows the debs find him fascinatingly bohemian, so he plays into it like simply anything. I shan't be taken in, of course, but I couldn't help compare him to all the Lord St Johns and Sir Cyrils and Honorable Horaces, and think how nice it would be to be an heiress, or even just a woman with a small private income, who could marry whomsoever she pleased and spend her Saturdays feeding seedcake to monkeys and making strings of paper dolls for little girls instead of entertaining dull middle-aged gentlemen at hunting lodges. I suspect I will be quite good at entertaining dull middle-aged men at hunting lodges, but Sebastian's wife, whoever is brave enough to marry him, will have a jolly sight more fun!

Have you met any young men yet, Polly? What about your Mr Thompson? Would he do? Is he good-looking? He sounds kind, which is not to be underrated in a husband. Uncle Simon is not always kind to Aunt Eliza – he does not hurt her, but he can be terribly cutting. Every time he does it, I think of Mummy and Daddy, and how sweet Daddy is to Mummy, and I promise myself that I will never marry someone who is not kind.

Write soon.

Yours practically,

Sophia

45 Park Lane
Liverpool
14th January 1897

Dear Tirzah and Sophia,

Ha!

Actually, Mr Thompson *is* quite good-looking. At least, he's kind-looking, which is sort of the same thing, I think, don't you? He is fearfully old, of course – he must be nearly *thirty*! And he always looks tired. I think he's in quite a lot of pain – his leg is all twisted round the wrong way, which looks horribly painful. And he doesn't sleep well. I don't think he does, anyway. I heard the housekeeper ask how he'd slept, and he pulled a sort of face. I think she worries about him. All the staff do. We all like him a tremendous amount. I don't think he gets enough to eat; he always looks thin and pale. I asked him about it, and he said sometimes he is so tired he's unable to eat anything, which horrified me. I berated him about it most soundly.

'You need a wife,' I told him, and he pulled another face.

'I barely have time to answer my letters, let alone go courting!' he said. 'And what wife would want to live in a dusty old orphanage?'

But I don't think the orphanage is dusty at all. There is always something happening, and the children are such funny dears, even the ones who are clearly very unhappy and angry. I would not work in an ordinary school now if you paid me double.

Our orphanage does need more money, though. Mr Thompson is always trying to think of ways to raise funds. I told him he should ask the local churches, but he said they are so concerned with morality, which is a problem when he wants to give a home to all the children who need it, not just those whose parents were married. Mr Thompson does not believe in passing the sins of the father onto the child, and I must say I think he's quite right.

I told him he should use the local women. Women's lives are so empty. We are not allowed to work, not allowed to study, we spend our lives sitting around and going for walks, and playing tennis and croquet and golf, reading improving novels, and going out for tea. Mother says the Empire is run by committees of women. She herself is on several church ones, an amateur dramatics society committee and a committee to provide every child in the parish with a toy at Christmastime. (All right, I made up the last one.) But women have a great deal of energy and kindness, and unmarried women so often have nowhere to put it.

Mr Thompson looked a bit taken aback and said that because he already had the trustees to deal with, he didn't think he could cope with another committee in his life. But I explained that the women wouldn't have to be on a committee. They could come and teach knitting or needlework to the older girls. Listen to the little ones read. Teach music and singing. Anything novel is a joy in our orphanage – their lives are so restricted, poor dears – and women are experts at filling empty days. We have to be!

His eyes lit up immediately.

'If they would come, we would love them,' he said. 'But I confess, I haven't the first idea where one finds such creatures. And' – his face fell rather comically as he said this – 'I don't know how I am ever going to find enough hours in the day to do so.'

He *does* need a wife. But it would have to be the right sort – someone genuinely interested in the children's welfare. I wonder how many worthy organisations survive on the unpaid work of wives. The church does, certainly – being a vicar's wife is a full-time job.

I don't think he would find it hard to find a wife, if he went looking. He is so kind, everyone likes him. And so clever and interesting. Maybe I shouldn't ask too many young women to come and teach the girls needlework – one of them might marry him instead! Oh, dear, I suppose I am guilty of making out women to be fit only to be helpmeets, which Miss Clearly was so against – do you remember? But his job is too much for one man, especially a man who is not well, and the orphanage cannot afford to pay for a housekeeper to take care of him, so a wife is his only option!

Maybe I'll marry a millionaire like Sophia, and then I'll pay for a lady superintendent to work alongside him, with a special commission to make sure he eats three meals a day and is not woken up in the middle of the night by catastrophes.

I must say, it would be fun to be rich, if only so you could give your friends bounteous presents. I would pay a handsome wage to one hundred families to adopt our children. I would give Mr Thompson a week by the seaside and a French chef to bring the colour back to his cheeks. I would pay for all your sisters to have as many Seasons as they need, Sophia, so you may marry your Sebastian. And I would set you up with a flat in Liverpool, Tirzah, and a maid, and buy you enough dresses that you could go dancing every night. It would be so jolly.

In other news, it's my eighteenth birthday next month. We are going to see *Much Ado About Nothing*, and to dinner, and there's going to be a tea party with games and charades. All my Liverpool friends are coming (though not Mr Thompson, of course!). But Anne, who works at the orphanage with me; and Peggy from down the road; my friends from church and the tennis club;

and Michael is coming down from Edinburgh for the weekend.

Do you think you girls might be able to come too? Are girls allowed a weekend off from the Season, Sophia? Would your grandmother say yes, Tirzah? Mother said to tell you that she is happy to write to your grandmother if you think that would help. But then, she used to let you come for Christmases without writing, didn't she?

I remain, your worldly friend,

Polly

P.S. I think your Sebastian sounds like a duck, Sophia. About as far from a dull landowner as one could possibly get!

Bannon House
Abyford
Perthshire
17th January 1897

Dear Polly and Sophia,

Polly, I cannot tell you how much I would *love* to come to your birthday. The theatre! A tea party! Other girls! It is like a dream of Elysium. And honestly, if I were my grandmother, I'd put me on the first train and tell me to stay till Tuesday. She's always complaining about my moaning and whining; how I do not do even the simplest tasks without making a meal of it, and how a young girl is supposed to be the light of a house, not a hag bringing everyone else down with her moaning.

She's in a foul mood today, but perhaps she'll be all right tomorrow. We'll see. I'm not hopeful, though. She never says yes to anything if she thinks it might bring me even the smallest bit of pleasure.

Yours pathetically,

Tirzah

Wimpole Street
London
19th January 1897

Dear Polly and Tirzah,

I'm sure I can come, Polly. If Aunt Eliza won't allow it, Mummy and Daddy will. They know how important you are. It's only a weekend, after all!

A rather miserable day here, though I try not to let it bother me. Isabelle was taken to court to be presented to Queen Victoria.

Naturally, as a poor relation, I could not expect such patronage (and nor did I). And I certainly don't have any gowns suitable for such a grand occasion. Still, I could not help but be a little downhearted about the whole thing.

I tried not to let it show, and made all the right noises, oohing and ahhing over Isabelle's dress (which was extremely beautiful) and her hair and her shoes and all that. Isabelle of course was an absolute cat about the whole thing. 'It is such a shame *you* cannot come, Sophia.' Or 'Imagine how *you* would look at the presentation in one of *your* homemade dresses! The Queen would die of laughter!'

She is a beast. I think Aunt Eliza was quite shocked. 'If I hear any more of that, Isabelle, I shall take that dress off you and send Sophia in your place. At least she is a polite, helpful child, unlike some I could mention!' Goodness! Aunt Eliza does not usually come in on my side. It did shut Isabelle up, though.

Anyway, so that took up most of a week in preparation and dissection and celebration. And then I went to a dance at Lord St John's house and danced six dances with him, and he was perfectly correct and dull as Sunday prep and . . . Oh, I know I am very lucky to be here at all, but golly, girls, it is hard being a poor relation sometimes! Why are all the eligible men so boring? The ones who are interested in me, anyway. The interesting, handsome ones of course have their pick of the girls and wouldn't look twice at a poor relation in a homemade ball gown. Still! I would rather be me than Isabelle any day. But please do write to me at once and tell me you love me so I don't feel quite so second-rate.

Your disheartened friend,

Sophia

45 Park Lane
Liverpool
22nd January 1897

Dear Sophia and Tirzah,

Of course we love you, darling Sophia. Who wants to be presented to the silly old Queen, anyway? I heard court presentations are always a fearful crush and she looks like a frightful bore to me, all double-chinned and grumpy. I wager you had a jollier time of it at home than Isabelle did.

Nothing so exciting as a court presentation is happening to me, but I do have some news. I asked Miss Martin about my three little boys, and it turns out they are quite correct! Well, about the stepmother, at least. Miss Martin says she turned up at the orphanage and said she simply couldn't look after them and had no reason to do so, as she is not a blood relation, so the orphanage must take them. Miss Martin says she and Mr Thompson tried to reason with her – we are so full that places must really go to children who would otherwise be sent to the workhouse or left on the streets. But Miss Martin says she simply walked off and left them there, without so much as a goodbye!

I asked Miss Martin about her, and she said she was a piece of work. The children were hungry, and their shoes were falling apart, but the stepmother was well-dressed and seemed quite content. We do get children from families that cannot afford to feed them, quite a lot of the time, but usually the mother is the hungriest, or else it is all going on drink, or worse.

I asked about the father, and Miss Martin said he was dead. But of course she only has the stepmother's word to go on. What if the stepmother were lying?!

I know, it's a bit far-fetched. But I can't stop thinking about it. Daragh seemed so sure he was alive. What if she abandoned them at the orphanage and told their father they had died? Or didn't tell their father what had happened to them at all? People put other people in asylums all the time – or they do in books, anyway. Why should an orphanage be any different? I don't suppose the boys know his address in India – they might not even know his regiment. They wouldn't know how to contact him.

And if what she said were true – well, someone should tell poor Daragh about it. The child is determined his father will come back and claim him, and if he never will, someone should tell him gently and kindly. It will break his heart if he doesn't appear.

I am going to talk to the boys about it again next time I see them, and try to work out what really happened. They must know their father's name, if not his regiment. I didn't tell Miss Martin for fear she would think me ridiculous, but I know you will understand.

Your loving but slightly foolish friend,

Polly

P.S. Birthday invitations are enclosed! You can of course both have a bed at our house. I do hope you can come!

YOU ARE CORDIALLY INVITED TO

Mary Anniston's 18th birthday party

ON

5th-7th February 1897

Arrivals on 5th February, followed by a quiet evening at home. Afternoon tea and games at 45 Park Lane from 2 p.m., 6th February, followed by *Much Ado About Nothing* at the Empire Theatre. Carriages on the morning of 7th February.

R.S.V.P.

45 Park Lane, Liverpool

Rat-infested dungeon
Perthshire
25th January 1897

Dear Polly and Sophia,

Well, I asked Grandmother about your invitation, Polly, but no luck. I confess, I am not surprised. I think she has realised that perhaps I would not come back. I probably wouldn't. Do they need any more teachers in your orphanage? Although, let's be honest, I would be a terrible teacher. I *am* a terrible companion. I cannot even type. I am fit for nothing but marriage. I would be a good wife to a wealthy gentleman who wanted a bit of fun when he came home. All he would have to do would be to take me to dances and the theatre and promise we never have to see my grandmother again.

I wish I knew what Grandmother had against fun. How many times do we sing 'Rejoice!' and 'Alleluia!' in church? It can't be sinful if it's in a hymn, can it? Perhaps she didn't realise Polly is short for Mary and thought I was making you up. Maybe she thinks I'm really running away to join the circus. I wish I was.

Anyway, don't worry, I think I can arrange your party. I will probably get into frightful trouble for it, but I don't care. It will be worth it.

Yours, filled to the brim with girlish glee (or is it plotting?!!),

Tirzah

Wimpole Street
London
27th January 1897

Dear Polly and Tirzah,

Tirzah, what are you plotting? Are you going on the streets? Robbing a bank? Should we be worried?

Some argy-bargy here too – my coming means I will miss a party that is apparently terribly important – I don't care, though. You're more important than some Mayfair party, Polly, even if it *is* a party that's being held by a minor earl. I bet you didn't know you could have minor earls, did you? Well, you can. And then such a fearful lot of fuss about my going on the train alone, which is absurd. Heaven knows what they would say if they knew you bicycled to your orphanage every day, Polly! It is so strange, because half of these girls live on country estates in the middle of nowhere and spent their whole childhoods roaming the woods, jumping in ditches, chasing foxes over hedges on horseback, and generally doing far more dangerous things than getting a train to Liverpool. But there you go. I don't think Aunt Eliza likes to acknowledge that Liverpool is a real place, and Uncle Simon only knows about it because of the Grand National. But then Mummy wrote and said of course I must go, and so it is all arranged. I shall be arriving at Lime Street station on the 18.57!

Your excited friend,

Sophia

45 Park Lane
Liverpool
28th January 1897

Dear Sophia,
Hurrah!

Dear Tirzah,
Please don't do anything stupid.
Polly

A rocky outcrop in a
desert land
Illuminated with a single
ray of light, which is your
invitation
31st January 1897

Dear Polly and Sophia,

All is arranged! I shall be on the 16.47. Please do send someone to meet me, as I'm not sure I have the money to pay for a hansom cab.

Tirzah

Dear Grandmother,

I have run away. Don't worry, not permanently. I shall be back home on Sunday morning. Expect me on the 9.37 from Edinburgh.

I haven't stolen the money for the train tickets, before you call the police. I pawned Aunt Lucy's silver locket that you said I could have from her jewellery box. I did it last week at the shop on the high street in Perth, if you want to get it back. I don't. It was an awful necklace. The pawnshop owner thought so too. He ummed and ahhed before he would give me anything at all for it. I had to give him the carriage clock from my bedroom and Grandfather's silver watch and chain too. I wasn't sure how much money pawnbrokers gave you, so I thought I'd better bring them too, just in case.

I am going – as you can hardly fail to have guessed – to Polly's eighteenth birthday in Liverpool. Please do not pursue me, unless you want the whole party to know that I am uncontrollable and unmanageable. I shall not tell you the address, but you probably have it somewhere in your writing desk if you care to discover it.

Do not worry – it is a perfectly respectable party. Though I do not deceive myself that you refused me from any care for my safety. You were perfectly happy for me to spend the Christmas and Easter holidays with Polly when I was at school. Did you know they took me out for tea every half-term holiday for the last five years? I don't suppose you did. You never asked. But you do understand why I can't miss Polly's eighteenth birthday party, don't you? I owe her so much. And a girl only turns eighteen once in her life.

In case you have forgotten, I shall remind you that Polly's father is a doctor, and her mother's father was a vicar. And they all are dears.

I shall be back on Sunday. Punish me all you like then.

Your regrettable granddaughter,

Tirzah

FROM: LIVERPOOL LIME STREET
TO: BANNON HOUSE, ABYFORD

ARRIVED SAFELY AT STATION STOP MET POLLY'S FATHER STOP HE PAID FOR THIS TELEGRAM STOP WASN'T THAT GENTLEMANLY OF HIM. TIRZAH

A mysterious location
somewhere in
Liverpool
6th February 1897

Dear Grandmother,

Well, I am here. And I am not dead, you will be pleased to note. The train journey was fine, though rather cold. The other travellers had blankets, but I forgot to bring one. However, a very nice lady let me share hers from Edinburgh, so it wasn't so bad.

I wasn't going to write, but then I thought perhaps you might blame Sarah for my going, and it wasn't her fault at all. I told her you had sent me into Perth to do the shopping and that I would be late because you had agreed to let me go to a lecture at the Baptists' Hall. I wasn't sure she would buy it, since you never let me do anything, but she did. It was all my fault and nobody else's – except, if you will excuse me from mentioning it, your own. If you only treated me as other girls are treated, I should not need to tell you lies and hide things from you.

Anyway. I am having a simply scrumptious time. We are going to the theatre this evening in our best dresses – I do not have a best dress, of course, so I am going in the object I used to wear at school for dancing lessons. It was that or my Sunday dress. But fortunately my friend Sophia has lent me a darling little bolero jacket and a silk flower to put in my hair, so it has come off better than it might have done.

Everyone was so kind when I arrived. They all wanted to know my news, and about life in Abyford. They were quite shocked when I told them I go nowhere and see nobody! Are you ashamed of yourself – shocking the good gentlefolk of Liverpool? It's a pity, because otherwise I think I came off rather well. We had a tea party at home this afternoon. It was ever so jolly! We had games and music – my singing was much complimented, which I mention not to boast but to show you that I am not fit for nothing.

Polly works as a teacher in an orphanage, did you know? See how respectable she is. Wouldn't you like to think that your granddaughter was doing good in the world like that too?

I suppose I shall arrive home before this letter does. (I'd forgotten about it being Sunday tomorrow.) Oh well. I shall post it anyway. I would like you to know what my party was like, and I don't suppose you'll listen to me in person.

Your very happy and not-at-all-sorry granddaughter,

Tirzah

45 Park Lane
Liverpool
8th February 1897

Dear Tirzah and Sophia,

Thank you SO MUCH for coming! I had the most wonderful time! Sophia, you looked so sophisticated! All the girls thought your dresses and hair were simply ravishing – you looked like quite a different person! However did you learn to do it? It wasn't just the clothes, it was – oh, everything! I felt so proud to know you.

Tirzah, darling, it was SO good to see you. About the thing we talked about – I asked Mother, and she said that if your grandmother could spare you, she would love to have you come and live with us. 'I do miss having a full house when everyone's away at school!' she said, although really, with Betsy and me and the little children, it is not exactly empty. So do ask her, darling. The little ones' governess has just left, so there would even be work for you to do, if you wanted it. How do you feel about wiping faces and supervising prep and taking the children to morning school?

I do hope your grandmother is not too angry with you. Please write back soon and tell us how you are.

Polly

Wimpole Street
London
11th February 1897

Dear Polly and Tirzah,

Thank you *so much* for the weekend, Polly! I had such a lovely time, I can't tell you! And honestly, it is all just stage dressing. Hair and skin and clothes and so forth. We spend most of our afternoons, when we are not at tea parties, primping and preening ourselves. It is very dull. But it does work.

I don't think I had realised quite how *tiring* it is being the poor relation all the time. The first week I was there, I made so many mistakes. Little things, like saying 'notepaper' instead of 'writing paper' and not knowing whether girls were allowed to drink wine or not, and dancing a waltz 'like a child at dancing school', as one man apparently said to Aunt Eliza, very cuttingly. Well, where else were we supposed to learn to dance? We are all seventeen and eighteen-year-olds, after all.

Anyway, Polly, it was so lovely to be somewhere where nobody cares how much money your father has, or how many dresses or admirers you have. The Season may be rather glorious fun – and it *is* fun – but it isn't anywhere near as nice as sitting around your drawing room fire toasting crumpets with you and Tirzah and Michael and your little brothers and sisters. I do like your family. And I like your friends too. It's lovely to meet them in person after hearing so much about them! It was so nice to be with sensible, ordinary people who just like to have a jolly time playing charades and eating cream buns, and who know what it's like to have to save money for the omnibus home. The Season is a wonderful whirl, but it is not real life. (Though perhaps the children in your orphanage would have felt the same about your party. That's a funny thought, isn't it?)

My favourite part, though, was when everyone had gone home, and we were all together in your bedroom, just like we used to be at school. I am so glad Alice and Charlotte were still away at school so we could share a bedroom just like we used to! Letters are wonderful things, but they aren't the same as seeing you in person.

Tirzah, what on earth did your grandmother say when you got home? Are you being punished? I half expected her to show up at the party, like Banquo's ghost, waving her walking stick (does she have a walking stick?) and pointing at you.

I'm so glad you came. It wouldn't have been the same without you.

Missing you already,

Sophia

Bannon House
Abyford
Perthshire
13th February 1897

Dear Polly and Sophia,

Well! I am in such trouble, I can't tell you. I don't care, though. It was worth it.

I told Grandmother which train I was on, and I did wonder if she might come to meet me, but she didn't. She did send a fly though to collect me from the station, so that was something.

When I got home, Sarah opened the door, looking frightened.

'There you are, miss!' she said. 'Where have you been, you naughty girl?'

'You know perfectly well where I've been, and so does Grandmother,' I said.

'You'd best go in and see her,' Sarah said, looking nervously over her shoulder. 'She's that angry, miss.'

She was. She didn't strike me or anything like that, but she was just coldly furious. I have been locked in my bedroom since Sunday night, and she is not going to give me any more allowance. I have to write lines, if you can believe that! Lines!

I don't know how long I am supposed to stay in here. Probably for ever. I don't care. It is better than reading Waverley novels to Grandmother. Although it *is* rather lonely. Still, it was worth it just to have those two days with you. We did have a jolly time, didn't we?

I wish I could come and live with you, Polly, but I don't think it's likely right now. I'm not sure my grandmother will even let me go into town, let alone move to Liverpool.

I love you both so much.

Tirzah

I must not go anywhere without Grandmother's permission
I must not go anywhere without Grandmother's permission
I must not go anywhere without Grandmother's permission
I must not go anywhere without Grandmother's permission
I must not go anywhere without Grandmother's permission
I must not go anywhere without Grandmother's permission
I must never lock any granddaughters I might have in their bedrooms, no matter what they've done
I must not go anywhere without Grandmother's permission
I must not go anywhere without Grandmother's permission
I must not go anywhere without Grandmother's permission
I must not go anywhere without Grandmother's permission
I must be a loving mother and grandmother, listen to my children, and not try to control them
I must not go anywhere without Grandmother's permission

I must not go anywhere without Grandmother's permission
I must not go anywhere without Grandmother's permission
I must not go anywhere without Grandmother's permission
Are you even reading these?
I must not go anywhere without Grandmother's permission
I must not go anywhere without Grandmother's permission
I am not a child, you know. School stops asking you to write lines when you hit the upper fifth.
I must not go anywhere without Grandmother's permission
I must not go anywhere without Grandmother's permission
I must not go anywhere without Grandmother's permission
I must not go anywhere without Grandmother's permission
I must not go anywhere without Grandmother's permission
I must not go anywhere without Grandmother's permission
I must go everywhere without Grandmother's permission

I only get one life. And it's mine, not yours. It's a sin to waste it.

I must not go anywhere without Grandmother's permission

I must not go anywhere without Grandmother's permission

I must not go anywhere without Grandmother's permission

I must not go anywhere without Grandmother's permission

I must not go anywhere without Grandmother's permission

I must not go anywhere without Grandmother's permission

God, I'm so bored.

I must not go anywhere without Grandmother's permission

I must not go anywhere without Grandmother's permission

I must not go anywhere without Grandmother's permission

I must not go anywhere without Grandmother's permission

In three and a half years, I will be twenty-one.

I must not go anywhere without Grandmother's permission

I must not go anywhere without Grandmother's permission

I shall not need your permission to do anything then.

I must not go anywhere without Grandmother's permission

I must not go anywhere without Grandmother's permission

I'll be able to go and be a chorus girl, or a streetwalker, or anything, and you won't be able to stop me.

I must not go anywhere without Grandmother's permission

I must not go anywhere without Grandmother's permission

I think a chorus girl's life would be rather jolly. And they are always marrying earls – in books, anyway.

I must not go anywhere without Grandmother's permission

I must not go anywhere without Grandmother's permission

I just want what everyone else has. A normal, happy life. A husband. A family.

I must not go anywhere without Grandmother's permission

I must not go anywhere without Grandmother's permission

I must not go anywhere without Grandmother's permission

I must not go anywhere without Grandmother's permission
I must not go anywhere without Grandmother's permission
I must not go anywhere without Grandmother's permission
I must not go anywhere without Grandmother's permission
I must not go anywhere without Grandmother's permission
I think I hate you.
I must not go anywhere without Grandmother's permission
I must not go anywhere without Grandmother's permission
You cannot actually force me to write these, you know?
I must not go anywhere without Grandmother's permission
I must not go anywhere without Grandmother's permission
I have my fingers crossed behind my back. You should know that.
I must not go anywhere without Grandmother's permission
I must not go anywhere without Grandmother's permission
I shall escape. I don't know quite how yet, but I shall.

I must not go anywhere without Grandmother's permission
I must not go anywhere without Grandmother's permission
They told us at school that it was a sin to hate anyone.
But they hadn't met you.

45 Park Lane
Liverpool
14th February 1897

Dear Mrs Lewis,

I hope you will forgive the impertinence of my writing to you like this. But I just wanted to tell you how charmed we all were by Tirzah at my daughter's eighteenth birthday celebrations. She is such a lively and vivacious girl, so well-mannered and grateful for all the attention. And her singing voice is truly remarkable. I know she had lessons at school – does she manage to keep up her singing at home? I hope so. A truly accomplished adolescent is a rare thing indeed, as I know from sad experience. My Polly has quite given up the piano since coming home, and while we are very fond of her attempts at drawing and painting, nobody could claim they have the remotest artistic merit. Fortunately, her interests lie more towards philanthropy.

Tirzah behaved impeccably the whole time she was with us, and we were so sorry to see her go. I wondered – we have taken a house on the Isle of Man for July and August, and we would see it as a great privilege if you would allow Tirzah to accompany us. Polly's orphanage school will have broken up, and though she is a great help with her younger brothers and sisters, it would be a kindness to her to have a friend with her.

I hope you will forgive me if I say that a young girl like Tirzah needs some fun and pleasure in her life. I am sure that there are many girls who are well-suited to a quiet life as a housekeeper, but I am not convinced that Tirzah is one of them. I believe if she were allowed the opportunity, she might well make a most advantageous match – she is an attractive child, as I'm sure you know. Perhaps I overstep my place, but I do not believe she is happy.

With my eldest son, Michael, away at university, we have a spare room at our house, which we would be delighted to offer to Tirzah, and I'm certain I could find some suitable employment for her here in Liverpool. She was a great success with my youngest children, and I know the orphanage where Polly works is crying out for more gentlewomen to help.

I remain, your obedient servant,

Sylvia Anniston (Mrs)

Bannon House
Abyford
Perthshire
15th February 1897

Dear Mrs Anniston,

Thank you for your kind offer. I regret that I cannot spare my granddaughter for the summer – since she has come home, I have let my companion go, and Tirzah's services are required here.

If I may offer you some advice in turn – it is extremely ill-mannered to comment on another person's choices for their dependents. I wonder that you did not realise it. How I choose to raise my granddaughter is my own business, and I would prefer if you did not contact me again.

Your obedient servant,
Moira Lewis (Mrs)

Flat 4A Ferguson
Buildings
Jackson Street
Edinburgh
15th February 1897

Dear Miss Lewis,

I hope you don't consider it any impertinence my writing to you. Polly gave me your address and said you were having rather a rough time of it at the moment. And if I may say so, your grandmother sounds like an absolute demon! Would you like me to ride up to your window and carry you away?

I did so much enjoy talking to you at Polly's party. Polly is a dear, but her friends do tend to be rather earnest reforming types, so it was especially jolly to see you and Sophia again. Your face when all those cakes came in for the birthday tea! You looked like a workhouse child at Christmas. I never saw a girl enjoy a cream cake so much. So many act as though it's a crime to enjoy eating, which I think is a shame. I like a good cream cake myself.

I'm sorry – I am rambling. I don't write many letters to girls (my sisters don't count), so I'm not sure what to say. How are you? I am fine. That's the sort of thing, isn't it? Well, I hope you are not too lousy. I am tolerably well.

I am supposed to be memorising all the bones in the arm, but you are far more interesting.

Oh! Compliments! That's the other thing one's supposed to put, isn't it? How fine your eyes are, and all that. Well, I'm not sure we're quite at the stage in our relationship where I feel able to describe your eyes, but if you do happen to want to know what I think of them, please reply as soon as you can bear to,

your nervous admirer,

Michael Anniston

Wimpole Street
London
17th February 1897

Dear Sebastian,

I am so angry with you, I could scream. How *dare* you behave to me like that last night? To propose like you meant it, on one knee, like this wasn't all a silly game? Frivolous one minute, deathly serious the next? Are you playing with me? You haven't given the first thought to how you would support me. You knew I must reject your proposals, and knowing that, I think it was cruel of you to make them.

And to answer your inane question (which I was polite enough to ignore in your last letter, though it made my blood boil) what my father thinks about 'marrying for money' is none of your business. Even if I did have an entirely free choice about the matter, I wouldn't marry a man whose only plan for his life is to idle it away at parties, living off the patronage of those who think he's funny. And what about children? How were you intending to feed and educate them?

Please do not write or speak to me again.

Sophia

Wimpole Street
London
17th February 1897

Dear Polly and Tirzah,

Oh, Tirzah! I would like to slap that grandmother of yours, I really would. You can come and be a hermit in my grand country estate, if I ever get one.

I am wretched. That damned fool Sebastian proposed to me yesterday. Properly, I mean – down on one knee and all that, like he meant it. He's always said he wanted to marry me, but I thought he understood that I couldn't. I thought it was at least mostly in jest.

Well, it wasn't. He was horribly serious – he did a whole speech in the arbour at Lord and Lady Stephen's garden party. And – oh, just for a moment, I almost believed it. I imagined the two of us living in that flat of his parents', every day charming and absurd, and me never having to pretend to care about thoroughbreds again. And then—

Then I wanted to hit him. Because of course I can't marry a man who has no means of providing for me. And I *hated* that he thought this was something to joke about – when to me it was – was—

Well. A man who behaves like a child, when you are a girl of eighteen who is trying against all her inclinations to behave like an adult, is not an endearing prospect, let me tell you. I suddenly felt more lonely than I ever have in my life. I said, 'Oh, damn you – *damn* you—' and I turned around and walked back to the party. I hope he never speaks to me again.

Yours in wretchedness,

Sophia

Cell Number 4
Grandmother's Gaol
Abyford
Perthshire
17th February 1897

Dear Michael,

Goodness, I don't think it's an impertinence! I am a very forward girl, you know. I never had anyone to teach me how to behave. I am, frankly, delighted.

You probably don't know it, but I'm in fearful trouble for coming to Polly's birthday party. I didn't exactly get Grandmother's permission, you see. It was worth it, though. I felt like my feet didn't touch the ground once! *Now*, of course, they have come down to earth with the most fearsome crash. I have been locked in my room by my grandmother. So you must write back at once before I succumb to despair.

I'm glad you are well. I am well physically (I'm very healthy) but wretched emotionally.

And I simply long to know what you think of my eyes. I thought your eyes were excellent. (Do boys want to know what girls think of their eyes? Yours are lovely, but your hair is even nicer – all thick and dark and wavy, just like Polly's.)

Write back as soon as you absolutely can.

Tirzah

45 Park Lane
Liverpool
18th February 1897

Dear Sophia and Tirzah,

Oh, Sophia. I am so sorry. I wish you were still here so I could pet you and comfort you properly. Aren't men the absolute worst? And Tirzah, your grandmother is an absolute hag. Mother was incensed when she heard about your life. I didn't want to tell you, but she wrote to her asking if there was anything we could do to help. Mother says she sent back the most horrible letter. She was quite upset about it. But anyway, no luck.

I have been busy here too. I talked to the boys again. I had to wait a week until I was back on playroom duty, but when I came in, there they were, playing with Nicholas.

Their father's name is Sergeant Eoin O'Flannery – it's pronounced Owen, but written Eoin; they were very keen to explain that – and they don't know which regiment he's in, but he was based in Calcutta. They all knew that. I asked if they had any letters from him, but they don't. They don't have anything at all from their old life. Imagine, not even giving those children a letter from their father to cherish!

I asked if their stepmother had told them he was dead, if they remember getting a telegram or a letter, but they don't. They just remember her gathering them up one day and taking them to the orphanage.

'We told her Daddy would be back for us,' said Robert.

'What did she say?' I asked, and they all looked a bit subdued.

'She said we'd never see Daddy again,' said Daragh.

'But she didn't say he was dead?' They shook their heads.

Maybe I'm lucky – I don't know many monsters. But it seemed to me astonishing that this woman wouldn't have told the children if he'd died. Not to tell them is just so – so *callous*. But maybe some people are like that.

We see many children here whose mothers and fathers hit them, or ignore them, or neglect them. But even the worst parents, strange though it is to say, love their children. They want to do what's right for them, even if they aren't capable of it. But this . . . this *coldness* . . .

It made me shiver all over.

Anyway. I told them I would talk to Mr Thompson about it and try to get to the bottom of what had happened. But that immediately set them off into a panic. I was not to tell Mr Thompson anything, nothing at all. Not that their father might be alive, not that their stepmother was a coldhearted ogre, nothing, nothing.

'But why?' I said, genuinely confused.

Everyone likes Mr Thompson. Why were they so frightened of him?

'He's in league with her!' said Daragh. I admit, I nearly laughed out loud. But they insisted.

It turns out, when she first brought them to the orphanage, she'd had some sort of a private meeting with Mr Thompson. She was in there a long time; I don't know what she said. But then she left, and he came out and told them they were to stay at the orphanage.

'We told him our father was still alive!' said Daragh in a fury. 'But he wouldn't believe us! He said he was dead and that we were to stay here for ever! I hate him! She's paying him to keep us here!'

I don't believe Mr Thompson would do something like that. He takes donations from kind civilians, of course, but he doesn't take money from monsters to keep children away from their loving parents. But naturally, I could see how the children would hate the man who told them their father was dead, and they are passionately insistent that he and their stepmother are in league with each other. Daragh said, 'Promise you won't talk to him. Promise! Or we shall never speak to you again!'

So then of course I had to promise. I swore it on my life and the lives of my brothers and sisters. (I knew they would like that; they are so devoted to one another.)

So. I wonder how many Sergeant Eoin O'Flannerys there are in Calcutta. And how does one find out where they are?

I wish I had military relations, but Annistons are all doctors and vicars or Merchant Navy types, alas.

Your top-secret sleuth of a friend,

Polly

Bannon House
Abyford
Perthshire
19th February 1897

A birthday party, two proposals, and a monkey! Some girls get ALL THE LUCK.

Tirzah

P.S. I'm sorry. I know it's pretty wretched for you. But honestly! I would cut off my right arm for even one suitor, and you have three!

P.P.S. I am still stuck in solitary confinement. I might go on hunger strike. I'd do it too, if meals weren't the only interesting thing that happens here.

Flat 4, Marsh Mansions
Haydown Street
Bloomsbury
London
19th February 1897

My darling Sophia,

I am wretched. I deserve every word you wrote to me and more. I would apologise again, but it feels rather redundant – I always seem to be apologising. You must get so tired of correcting me.

You're right that I've been treating this courtship as a sort of game. At least – I suppose that must be how it seems to you. Perhaps it started that way a little for me too. But over the weeks, my feelings for you have grown and solidified into something much stronger and more certain than I've ever known before. My life, as you must know, has always had something of the joke about it. Nobody in my family ever takes anything very seriously, and somehow things always come out all right. That's what happens when you have wealthy connections – I can hear your voice in my head, telling me so, and you are of course entirely correct.

I never expected you to marry me; you're right. But I also never really expected you to care very much for me at all. I've been attached to various women in my life, and it's never been very serious. Oh, we've professed our undying love to each other, naturally – I've been doing that with girls since I was eight years old – but none of us ever *meant* it.

I think you mean it. Or at least you would if you said it.

I think for the first time in my life, I mean it too.

It terrifies me, Sophia, honestly. You're quite right. I can't support you. I know you can't marry me. I caper around like a fool so I don't have to look at that directly and can pretend it's all a game. It isn't a game, though, is it?

This is the most honest letter I've ever written.

Perhaps it's best if you don't reply.

I wish you nothing but happiness.

Your friend, always,

Sebastian

Wimpole Street
London
20th February 1897

Dear Sebastian,

I hate you. Your letter made me cry. I hate you so much. Then I had to spend all afternoon at a beastly tea party with Aunt Eliza and my cousins, and the whole time I just wanted to *scream*.

You are one of the most fortunate people on the whole planet – the grandson of an earl, for heaven's sake! You have your health, your wits, your youth. And yet you sit around as though you're an invalid aunt, bemoaning your fate.

If I were a man, what wouldn't I do? If I didn't have my sisters to support, I mean. I used to think I'd be a journalist, but if I were a man perhaps I'd be a lawyer – or maybe I'd buy shares in a business. My father's brother owns a brewery – perhaps I'd go and work for him. I am so jealous of men who *make* things. Where I grew up, in Derby, they are always making things and building things and digging things up from the ground. It makes embroidered tablecloths and bonnets feel rather small beer in comparison. (I suppose women do make children. But it doesn't feel quite the same somehow.)

I want to shake you! Why, if you really care for me so very much as all that, don't you go off and do something about it? Get a job! You aren't entirely ridiculous; there has to be something you can do. Go on the stage if you must! You'd make a fine back end of a pantomime horse if nothing else.

You don't know how furious it makes me to watch you – you, who could be anything you want – sit there and wring your hands and say there is nothing to be done. If that's really what you think, well – well, you can't want it very much, that's all I can say.

Yours in scorn and rage,

Sophia

Wimpole Street
London
21st February 1897

Dear Polly and Tirzah,

Tirzah, you are an absolute ass, and if you can't say anything sensible, please just send a piece of blank paper in future.

I don't care, anyway. I put the dashing Sebastian out of my mind and danced four dances with Lord St John. He talked about nothing but fox-hunting and trout fishing, and I smiled the whole way through, though it made my jaw ache.

Yours sensibly,
Sophia

P.S. Sebastian did not show up at either of the parties we went to last week. I am GLAD GLAD GLAD GLAD GLAD.

P.P.S. I'm sorry, Tirzah, I know you don't mean it. I know I must look like a fairytale princess, while you are a poor Rapunzel, locked up in your tower. Maybe if you sing loudly enough out the window, you might attract a passing prince or two.

Flat 4, Marsh Mansions
Haydown Street
Bloomsbury
London
21st February 1897

Dear Sophia,

All right. I will.

Sebastian

P.S. If I got a job, would you marry me?

Wimpole Street
London
22nd February 1897

Dear Sebastian,

Don't be an ass.

Sophia

P.S. I might not hate you quite so much, though.

Flat 4A Ferguson
Buildings
Jackson Street
Edinburgh
22nd February 1897

Dear Tirzah,

I think your eyes are the nicest I've ever seen, if you really want to know. They sparkle when you're excited and when you're moved – it's like one can see your whole soul in them. That sounds more poetic than I meant it to, but I won't strike it out. I never knew a girl who opened so much of herself out to the world – and bear in mind, I speak as a gentleman with four younger sisters. Most girls are on their best behaviour in company – or at least, if not on their best behaviour, they're very *aware* that there's a gentleman present, if you see what I mean. They don't eat more than one cream cake, they don't go dancing jigs around the drawing room, when they laugh it's a nice feminine laugh, not a great delighted chortle like yours. You are the most *alive* person I know, and when I leave you, I feel like I am fizzing with electricity along all my nerve endings. You complete my circuits. There, that's what happens when you are romanced by a man of science! Do you like it?

Tirzah, has your grandmother really locked you in your bedroom, or were you exaggerating? How long is she planning on holding you there? Where are your parents? Do they know about this?

I know Polly worries about you. Please write back soon to your anxious admirer and reassure him that you are all right. In the meantime, I remain,

your friend,

Michael Anniston

Bannon House
Abyford
Perthshire
24th February 1897

Dear Michael,

Thank you for your letter. It was quite the nicest love letter I have ever received. Although – are you really sure you want to form an attachment with a girl who's made of electricity? It's all very well at a party, but it might get rather enervating in the long term. (I thought enervating meant over-exciting, but actually it means exhausting, did you know? I looked it up because I wasn't sure how to spell it. Still, I expect being attached to a lightning bolt would be exhausting as well.)

I don't think I'm an easy person to be with. The girls used to spend a lot of time at school comforting me when I'd done something foolish or got in another mess. I would love to be sensible and happy like Polly and Sophia (though Sophia isn't very happy at the moment, really). But I'm not sure it's in my nature. My life is always one catastrophe after another. I cannot cope without excitement. I don't know why.

I am out of my dungeon. I shall tell you how I got out if you promise not to tell the girls. I lay on my bed and screamed and screamed and screamed. I kept it up for hours. Grandmother was so furious. She wanted to gag me, but Sarah refused. Sarah is Grandmother's housekeeper. She said she wasn't going within five feet of me, and if Grandmother thought she was, she would give her notice. Sarah threatens to give her notice about once a month. It's gone up to about once a week since I came back home from school.

Grandmother took to sitting in the garden, but of course the neighbours could hear, and they came round and complained. Grandmother didn't like that. She doesn't like anyone to know that she's mistreating me. She also doesn't like to lose – she is fearfully stubborn – but in the end she had to do something. So she agreed that I could come out, but I would have to stay in the kitchen with Sarah and Cook and Minnie and do the washing up and polish the silver.

I didn't mind that. In fact, I rather liked it. I liked having something to do and people to talk to. Though Sarah, Cook and Minnie think I'm a wicked young limb who will no doubt come to a bad end, and took great delight in telling me so. But I didn't let that bother me. I found out lots of interesting things about their lives while I was down there. Cook is walking out with a carter called John Moore, who calls for her on her half-days and takes her for drives around the countryside in his cart. Imagine! Cook is hoping he will ask her to marry him, but he hasn't yet. Sarah doesn't think being married to a carter would be much fun because he'd be off all day and sometimes longer in his cart, and how would you know he wasn't getting up to mischief while he was away? But Cook said anything would be better than spending your whole life in a freezing attic with chilblains. I'm on Cook's side, obviously.

Minnie doesn't have a young man – she says she doesn't want one, they're more trouble than they're worth. On her half-day, she goes and visits her mother and helps do the baking. Minnie's mother worries about her in this big old house with just Cook to help with the work. She wants Minnie to get a job in a big hall with lots of other servants to rub along with. But Minnie says she isn't going to marry a footman, no matter what her mother thinks. She wants to see a bit of life first. I agree with this too, obviously. But I think it would be quite jolly to be a maid in a big servants' hall. I bet they get up to all sorts of things below stairs. There was a story in *Girl's Own* I read when I was at school about an earl's daughter who got a job as a maid because her father had lost all his money, and she ended up marrying the duke's son. Maybe I should do that. I got the silverware sparkling like anything.

As for my parents . . . I never knew my father. I don't even know his name. I think I'm probably illegitimate. Does that shock you? I know it wouldn't shock Polly or your mother, but they aren't paying court to me. There were several natural daughters of rich men at our school. You could stay in the holidays, you see, so it was quite a good place to park girls. Lots of children had parents in India and things.

I haven't seen or heard from my mother since I was seven years old. I don't know where she lives. I wrote her a letter once, but it came back saying she'd moved on.

Don't tell Polly that, will you? I never told her or Sophia, but I thought you ought to know if you're going to be sending me compliments about my eyes. I don't really think you'll mind, but could you write back quickly anyway, assuring me that you don't?

Your friend,

Tirzah

45 Park Lane
Liverpool
24th February 1897

To whom it may concern,

My name is Mary Anniston, and I am an employee of the Royal Liverpool Home for Orphans. I am trying to trace the father of three of our children, one Sergeant Eoin O'Flannery. The children could not remember his regiment, but they believe he was stationed in Calcutta, at least in 1895.

There is some confusion as to whether Sergeant O'Flannery is dead. It would be helpful if you could clear this up for us. And if he is not dead, could you please pass on his address to us here? Or, if that is not possible, inform him that we wish to communicate with him regarding his children, who are currently residents in our home.

Yours faithfully,
Mary Anniston

45 Park Lane
Liverpool
24th February 1897

Dear Tirzah and Sophia,

I found out a bit more about Mr Thompson today.

He was not at lunch, and although he could eat in his own quarters every day if he wanted to, he always makes a point to dine with the children and eat the same food they do, which I call very gentlemanly. (The food is plain but good, and there is plenty of it. Nobody goes hungry here, though they do eat rather a good deal of porridge, and bread and margarine, and the little ones do not get nearly enough milk. I know Mr Thompson worries about it.)

Miss Martin saw me looking and said, 'Oh! Mr Thompson is ill today, didn't you know? Matron said he must stay in bed all day today and tomorrow.'

'Why! What's wrong with him?' I said.

'Oh! He's often ill. I am sure he should not be running an orphanage if he is so unwell, but of course, it is so hard to find good people to work here, so we must take what we can get.'

'He *is* a good superintendent,' I said. He really is.

'Oh, indeed! But his health is very bad, you know. And I am sure he does not take proper care of himself.'

I am sure of this too – Mr Thompson seems to feel that he should have no more privileges than the children. It is very noble, but after all, the children who are sick do get better fires and food. I found I did not like to think of him being unwell, though it did not surprise me much. He does always look rather peaky, and he moves like he's in pain.

I wished I could think of something to help him, but of course I am very junior here in the establishment, and it is not my place to do anything. Fortunately, Mother had no such qualms.

'Oh, the poor dear man!' she said. She rang for Cook at once and insisted she make him a blancmange for me to take in tomorrow.

'I'm not sure what they will say if I bring in a blancmange to give to my superior, Mother,' I said, rather doubtfully.

'Tell them it came from Mrs Anniston and you had nothing to do with it,' said Mother in her firmest tone. It's hard to argue with Mother, so I decided to do as she said. And in truth, I was glad to have an excuse to do something for him. It's a miserable thing to be ill alone, particularly in a damp, dour building like our orphanage.

I gave the blancmange to Annie, the orphanage cook, who looked rather surprised but promised to pass it on to Mr Thompson. Heaven knows what he will think of it! Still, I suppose it is always good to know that someone cares about you, even if that someone is only the mother of your foolish friend,

Polly

My tower
Abyford
Perthshire
25th February 1897

Dear Polly and Sophia,

Rapunzel it is. Or it was. I am finally out of my room, thank goodness. I am still stuck in the middle of nowhere though. And my grandmother is certainly ogreish enough to fit the bill. What wouldn't I give for a prince to gallop to the rescue? If I had a granddaughter, I would want her to find a good husband for herself. Wouldn't you?

I don't suppose I shall ever have a granddaughter, or a daughter, or any child of my own. Aunt Lucy didn't. I always thought I would be a mother. That's something else my grandmother has taken away from me – my children. There must be thousands of women like Aunt Lucy and me, who are forced to spend their whole lives looking after their elders. Grandmother's sister had to stay at home and look after her parents too. It's such a queer thought, isn't it? Though I suppose we should consider ourselves lucky we are not being forced down mines or up chimneys. I think I would rather be a coal miner, though. At least there would be other people to talk to. I could marry a nice coaly gentleman and have lots of little coaly babies. I could welcome them all home at the end of the day and pop them in the bathtub, and then when they came out all sweet and clean and soapy, I could read them fairy stories.

There is a big book of fairy stories here in my bedroom. I think it used to be Mamma and Aunt Lucy's when they were children. There's a version of *Rapunzel* in it, but it's not quite the same one I remember.

The story of the mother who takes something from a garden is the same, but in this story it's parsley. And then the ogress (it's an ogress in this story, not a witch) takes the little girl away just the same and locks her in a tower. I never understood that part when I was small. The mother didn't know that she would lose her child, but she knew *something* bad was going to happen. I couldn't understand why she wouldn't just stop eating it.

And then the child gets stolen, and you never hear from the parents again. That part always bothered me too. The story says how much the couple longed for a child, and then they have to give her to the ogress, and she never sees them again. They never see her. At the end, when she marries the prince, is she the princess of the country where they live? Do they know their princess is their daughter? It's so queer. I hate it. I keep thinking about that mother and how sad she must be. Does she ever have another baby?

I always hated the part with the prince as well. Why couldn't she make a rope ladder and climb out of the window on her own? It's not difficult! I understand that part a bit better now. Where would she go? At least in the tower she has books and food and clothes. Is being in the forest all on her own with nowhere to go any better? I'm not sure I'd choose starvation over captivity.

I'm so lucky I have you two. I'm not alone. I do feel very alone here, though.

Anyway, in this Rapunzel story – only it's not Rapunzel, it's Petrosinella – Petrosinella doesn't get rescued, she runs away. And before she goes, she takes three nuts that are hidden on the shelf. The ogress follows after her, and each time she comes close, Petrosinella throws a nut after her and it turns into something different, like a bear or a donkey. The ogress defeats the first two animals, but the last one eats her up, and Petrosinella can go off with her prince.

I like that idea – of having special things that protect you. You were my first nut, Polly (you know you're a nut, and we love you anyway, so I hope you don't mind me calling you one). I ran away to your party, and I did secretly hope your mother and father might let me stay (though I didn't say so, of course, because I knew they wouldn't really). I know what my second nut is, but I'm going to have to wait before I throw this one. I'm not so hopeful about this one. It's not so solid as my first.

And then of course there's the prince.

Yours from the tower,

Tirzah

Flat 4A Ferguson
Buildings
Jackson Street
Edinburgh
25th February 1897

Dear Tirzah,

No, I don't despise you. How could I? It isn't your fault. I always thought that part in the Bible about the sins of the fathers being inflicted on the children was the most awful piece of beastly rot I ever read. You should just hear Polly talking about the adoptive parents who only want to take legitimate children from her orphanage! I expect you probably do. She never shuts up about it.

What was she like, your mother? Can you remember her?

All is well here. We are doing anatomy, which I thought would be horrible but is actually utterly fascinating. Does that horrify you? Whatever your childhood was like, at least you never cut up dead bodies. (Or rather I hope you didn't!)

I hope you don't mind that I like cutting up bodies. Or . . . 'like' is the wrong word. It isn't fun. But it is interesting. I think the world is such an interesting place, full of things to learn. For example, did you know there was a Dancing Plague in 1518, in Strasbourg? They say people danced until they died. Isn't the world a better place, just for knowing that?

Would your grandmother let me send you books? Do you like to read? I don't like reading as much as Polly does, but it might help with the boredom.

I am sending you a small present anyway to cheer your weary days. Make them last and remember your friend,

Michael

P.S. I am sending you a kiss – X! I hope you will not be offended. If you are, I will not send another.

Bannon House
Abyford
Perthshire
28th February 1897

Dear Michael,

You are a sweetheart. Your letter made me cry, but in a nice way. Things make me cry quite often nowadays, actually. Don't tell Polly.

Thank you for the comfits. How did you know I like them? They are a very superior sort. I am saving them. I suck one in the morning and one in the afternoon, and I think of you the whole time I am doing it.

I think of you a lot, you know. Your letters are quite the most interesting thing that happens to me here. Does it worry you that maybe I only like you because I am so desperate for attention? Don't worry, though – I think I would like you even if I were living in a whirl of gaiety, like Sophia.

I would love some books, yes, please. The girls send me things sometimes, and Grandmother never minds. If the book had a one-way ticket to Australia in it, that would be even better, but just a book would be lovely. Grandmother's books are all very dull. If I never read another Waverley novel again, I'll die happy.

I used to like you even when I came for Christmas in the holidays, do you remember? I used to flirt with you something rotten. I don't think your mother approved. She thought schoolgirls should be pigtailed rosy-cheeked innocents, more interested in hockey than boys. But lots of the girls at our school liked boys too. It's natural, isn't it? I bet boys at boys' schools like girls too.

I think anatomy sounds fascinating. I love it when people are interested in things. There was a girl in our form at school who knew everything there was to know about beetles, and the other girls used to quiz her about it sometimes, but I liked it. I always love Polly's letters where she talks about her job and the children. I wish everyone cared about what they do like that. I think you will too, won't you? You're like her in some ways, I think. You're kind and good-hearted and cheerful. Do you get to treat actual patients yet, or only dead ones?

I do remember my mother quite well, yes. My favourite memory of her is a summery one. We were walking down a street in Glasgow together – we lived in Glasgow – and there was a girl selling heather on the corner, and Mamma said, 'No, thank you,' and we walked past, but I kept looking back because the heather was so pretty. Mamma saw, and she stopped and turned round and bought a sprig and gave it to me, very solemnly, and said, 'Lucky heather for my best girl.' And I put it in my buttonhole and felt like the luckiest girl alive. I must have been about six. I remember thinking, 'I'll never forget this, not even when I'm one hundred.' And I never did.

I am going to send you two kisses back – XX. If that shocks you, I'm probably not the girl for you. Now you have to send me four, and I'll send you eight, and we'll end up with a pile of kisses so large, the page won't be able to hold them.

Your friend,

Tirzah

Wimpole Street
London
28th February 1897

Dear Polly and Tirzah,

Still no sight or sound of Sebastian. I am getting rather worried now. Perhaps the foolish boy really has decided to go and do something sensible with his life. Or perhaps he's gone off on a drinking and gambling binge to cheer himself up. Do men really do that outside of novels? And why don't women, do you think? I would quite like to go and lose all my money in the card-rooms of London, wouldn't you? So much more fun than having hysterics and ending up in a lunatic asylum.

Anyway, I am glad he has gone because it is forcing me to be practical. I have made a list of possible husbands.

1. George Carroll. Sorry, no.
2. Sebastian Fowler. Also, no. He is a darling, but too poor to tempt *me*. Alas!
3. Lord St John. A definite possibility. I think he would understand the terms of our agreement in a way that young Carroll perhaps would not. He would not ask too much of me (though I would, of course, be expected to provide children). I think we could live a very civilised sort of life together.

4. Ben Taylor. He's a younger son but not too shabbily off, I don't think. I rather like him, but I'm not sure he actually likes me. He is also very keen on the eldest Harmon girl. And Marigold Bently. And Winifred Davies. All right, not Ben Taylor. He is just a terrible flirt. And I don't really like him that much anyway.
5. Sir Percival. Yuck. He's about fifty. And a lech. No, thank you very much. I'm almost certain he tries it on with all the debs though, so I doubt very much any marriage proposals will be coming from *him*. And even if they did, I have my pride.

So all in all, St John looks the most likely. I shall put all thoughts of monkeys and charades and toasted muffins by the fireside out of my head and practise my smiles and my dancing with the man himself.

Yours, cheerful and practical,

Sophia

P.S. Polly, do you like Mr Thompson? I rather think you might. Maybe you should marry him. I could just see you helping him to run the orphanage.

45 Park Lane
Liverpool
2nd March 1897

Dear Tirzah and Sophia,

Oh! Mr Thompson would not want to marry me. He is a very clever man, you know – he has heaps of books on his shelves, most of them very serious tomes about child development and the proper management of orphanages. If he does marry, I expect he would like a serious sort of woman who could talk properly with him about grown-up sort of things, not a schoolgirl like me.

I took tea with him again today. It wasn't my turn, but he wanted to say thank you for the blancmange. I asked after him, and a message came down from on high telling me to go on up.

He was in his little sitting room – I was pleased to see he had a good fire, at least – resting in an armchair in his dressing gown and slippers. I felt quite maternal, seeing him there, looking so pale, with the account book open in his lap and all the receipts spread out on the floor around him. It wasn't how one usually conducts interviews with one's superintendent!

'I'm sorry, sir,' I said. 'Please don't feel you have to talk to me if you're unwell. I can come back another time.'

'It's no trouble,' he said. 'I've been tearing my hair out over these damned expenses, and I do feel rather as though I've been on the rack.'

He smiled at me. His smile is quite the nicest thing about him – warm and generous. It takes a special sort of person to give a smile that open even when they aren't feeling well. People who have too many cares are often selfish, aren't they? They don't have enough energy to spare for other people; it's all taken up with themselves. Some of the children are like that, especially the older ones. It is a gift to have enough time and space to care for others. That's a funny thought. Although one also sees people with nothing, especially women, who still give and give to those they love. There are so many children in our orphanage who are loved by aunts and grandmothers and sisters, who visit them on their half-days and worry about them and save up to buy them new shoes and little toys.

'I have been feeling rather lonely, shut up here by myself,' he said. 'It's nice to have a guest to tea. I promise I shan't talk about work if you would rather not.'

'Certainly not,' I said. 'In fact, I shall tidy all your account books away, so you shan't have to bother with it any more.' And I did. I gathered up all the bits of paper and receipts and put them in a pile by the door. Then tea arrived, and very plain it was too – just tea and bread and butter and day-old rock buns left over from the children's cookery classes. Not even any jam. 'What should we talk about instead?'

'Perhaps you could do the talking,' he said. 'My head aches rather too much to be witty and sparkling today.'

Well, at first I couldn't think what to say that would interest a clever gentleman like him, but once I'd started I found I couldn't stop. I told him about Mother making the blancmange, and then he asked about her, so I told him, and about Father, and all my brothers and sisters – that took rather a long time, but it made him laugh. He likes children, and I'm afraid our family was always rather more than usually naughty.

'It's nice to remember that there are happy children in the world,' he said.

I thought that was rather a funny thing to say. I never thought this place was the whole world. Just rather a sad corner of it.

'You need to leave the orphanage more often,' I told him, and he gave a rueful smile.

'When do I have the time for that?' he said.

I got quite vehement then. I told him Mother always says that you can't do a good job if you don't play as well as work. I said the children need as much of the outside world as possible to come into the orphanage. It is *their* whole world, but it shouldn't be, and if we can't take them outside of it (though I think we *should*), we should bring the world to them.

'Why,' I said, 'our scullery maid – Agnes – she came from a workhouse, and she knew nothing of the world. She could barely read – she'd never been to the theatre, or to a party, or eaten cake, or done any of the things a child should. Mother says –' I find myself quoting Mother a lot when I talk to him, but it is only because she speaks such good sense – 'that if you are to do a job well, you should know and experience as much as possible. You should read a newspaper every day, and go to concerts, and read poetry, and travel – I should love to travel, shouldn't you?'

I would like to bring the whole world to these children. Politics, theatre, philosophy. I would like to know more about those things myself too! I loved our school, you know I did, but we didn't learn any politics, or science, or economics, or anything that might not be suitable for a young lady to know. I only know the difference between the Tories and the Liberals because Michael told me. (Not that this knowledge is much *use* without a vote. But still!) Half of the women I meet in Mother's drawing room don't have the first idea about how the world is put together. And so many of the parents we meet here don't either. One woman had never heard of Glasgow, and another thought Disraeli was an Arabian prince!

I said all this to Mr Thompson, and he sat there in his dressing gown, smiling at me and looking almost human.

'The more life you find in the outside world, the more you will bring in to the children here,' I told him.

'I believe you are right,' he said. 'Though heaven knows where I shall find the time.'

I told him I would make him a bargain. I would find him some women from Mother's church to help him with the administration. And he must set aside a whole evening just for pleasure.

'May I spend it asleep?' he said, with a smile playing around his eyes – he really has the nicest smile I have ever seen.

'Certainly not,' I told him. 'You must go to the theatre – or the Walker Art Gallery – or a ferryboat on the Mersey – or walk in the park. I insist.'

'Well,' said he, 'if you can find me a woman willing to do my paperwork for nothing, I can give you an evening at the theatre.'

So we agreed.

He looked quite cheerful after this exchange – I think he likes to have someone to disagree with him – but he did look tired. So I said I would leave him to rest and report back.

'Aye-aye, nurse. I shall sleep better for the thought of someone else to write my blasted accounts, I tell you.'

When he said that, I had an idea. I gathered up the account book and the receipts and took them home with me. I'm going to work on them all evening and present him with the finished book tomorrow. Won't he be pleased?

Your invigorated friend,

Polly

Wimpole Street
London
2nd March 1897

Dear Louisa,

I know I do not write as often as a good sister should (though you never write to me either, so I don't feel you can take too much offence). However, I need your HELP. My current suitor – a certain Scottish lord, don't chewknow – is a fiend for horses and hunting, and of course I know nothing about it. He goes on and on about three-year-old geldings and brood mares and heaven knows what else. I've always considered myself reasonably intelligent, but I am flummoxed. What are you supposed to SAY when someone tells you about an animal that lives hundreds of miles away? Why are you supposed to care? HELP.

I know I always mocked you for spending so much time mucking out other people's stables – honestly, what sort of a hobby requires clearing up horse dung? – but it turns out perhaps it would have been useful to learn how to ride. Half the debs are mad keen on horses, of course. The ones with country estates, anyway. The London set roll their eyes a bit, but the men like it. Or some of them do.

How is school? Tell Mrs Mannering that she needs to add a class on Talking to Men – it would be much more useful than geography and history and arithmetic. Maybe she could organise a dance with the boys at the Grange School – wouldn't *that* be something?!

I do miss it, you know. School. I thought real life would be so – well, so glamorous. And it really is! But it's also . . . Well. More *real.*

Anyway. WRITE BACK SOON and tell me all about it. Do they still serve macaroons on Sundays? Does Mary Temple still step on your toes in dancing classes? Has anyone pulled any good pranks? Tell me all.

Your glamorous but disillusioned sister,

Sophia

Grangefield School for
Girls
Collingham
Derbyshire
5th March 1897

Dear Sophia,

Well, firstly, you can't pretend to be interested in horses. That would be idiotic. It would be like pretending to speak Japanese – you might get away with it to an onlooker, but a Japanese person would know in an instant.

I would tell him you're a total dunce but simply longing to learn. Do your usual thing of asking lots of questions and looking fascinated – you're good at that. Or else pretend to be very stupid and say 'Goodness, that sounds frightening! Aren't you brave?' But I wouldn't think that would work very well if he's already spent more than five minutes talking to you. So honesty is probably best. Except don't be too honest. Telling him you really think horses are smelly and stupid and ugly will get you nowhere. You must accept as natural law that horses are the most beautiful and fascinating creatures ever to walk the earth. If you do that, you should be all right.

School is school. It's not very exciting. Geometry and composition and prep and all that bore. I don't know why you're getting so nostalgic about it all of a sudden. Marrying a man with a herd of Arabian stallions – now that sounds like a dream!

Your practical and frankly envious sister,

Louisa

P.S. I hope you are not thinking of shirking your duty, you know.

The War Office
Cumberland House
Pall Mall
London
6th March 1897

Dear Miss Anniston,

My apologies for the delay in replying to your letter. I am afraid that without knowing Sergeant O'Flannery's regiment, we would be unable to trace him for you.

I wish you all the best in your search.

Yours sincerely,

John Talbot

Bannon House
Abyford
Perthshire
7th March 1897

Dear Polly and Sophia,

I agree with Sophia, Polly. You do like Mr Thompson, don't you? I could imagine you running an orphanage. It would be just the sort of job that would suit you. Ladies do run orphanages, don't they? But if you do, I think you should be paid for it. And I think whatever lady you find to do Mr Thompson's accounts should be paid for it too. I am basically an unpaid companion to Grandmother, and it is no fun at all. Just because we are ladies does not mean we should be taken advantage of.

I suppose you should marry St John, Sophia. But goodness, it does sound horribly grown-up and dull! Do you think Sebastian would consent to being a kept gentleman? You could buy him a flat in Paris and pay for his suits and visit him when your husband is off on fishing holidays.

I have some news, but I am not going to tell you what it is. It will probably come to nothing. But it is very nice to have it to hold on to. Don't worry, though, it is nothing dangerous or immoral. Your mother would quite approve, Polly. And Aunt Eliza would not be shocked.

I love you both so very much. Maybe we should all become kept women and live in a brothel together in Paris. Wouldn't that be jolly?

Yours immorally and immoderately,

Tirzah

Wimpole Street
London
11th March 1897

Dear Polly and Tirzah,

Tirzah, do I want to know? Please be careful. I know I am marrying for money, but I am doing so very carefully. If only you knew! I may be selling myself, but some prices are too high to pay.

Anyway, I have *news*. The plot thickens. Who should turn up at Aunt Eliza's At Home on Friday, but the Man Himself! Sebastian Fowler. Looking especially dashing in a new blue suit with a yellow silk tie and matching handkerchief in the pocket. The dear boy had made a special effort, and it did pay off! He was quite the nicest-looking man there. Though heaven knows where he found the money. I suppose he got it all on tick.

Anyway, he was clearly excited and nervous, and he made the round of the room while watching me all the time out of the corner of his eye and waggling his eyebrows at me, which made me laugh. He is such a comfortable person to be around! I could feel myself sort of filling up with happiness, like somebody was pouring it into me, just from knowing he was there. I *had* missed him. He is much the most entertaining person I know.

Eventually he made his way to me (I was stuck talking to Anthony Brunt, who is the most deathly bore imaginable), and he gave a little bow and waggled his eyebrows again, and he looked so happy, I just laughed, and he said 'Good news, cruel lady!' So I said 'What?' of course, and, well, it turns out he's actually gone and done it! He's got a job!

He's working as a secretary for Lord Winterbourne, who is a distant cousin of his – sorting out all his papers and answering his mail and organising his calendar and his events, that sort of thing. I suppose all those big parties must take a lot of planning. I couldn't believe it. 'But will you be able to *do* it?' I said. He doesn't strike me as the organised type. He pretended to take offence, but he was too happy to be really offended. 'I'll say!' he said. 'Our family takes a good deal of organising, you know. How do you think we manage to look so dashing on so little dough? All down to me, old thing – well, mostly me. I think it's about time the rest of the world got the benefit of my skills, don't you?'

'Well, naturally,' I said. I couldn't help but smile, he looked so pleased with himself. And of course I was glad he'd found himself some gainful employment – it really isn't good for a young man to be idle without the money to support it.

He seemed to enjoy having done it though, and I confess it does my heart good to think of him happily settled in useful employment. I did tell him I wouldn't marry him just because he'd got a job, but he didn't seem to mind. He kept hinting that he wanted another task, so since you girls are such experts in fairytales, perhaps you could suggest something for him. Perhaps I should ask him to find good matches for all four of my sisters – but of course he would have to wait until they were all of age, which might take rather an earthly long time.

Suggestions on a postcard, please, girls.

Your fairytale friend,

Sophia

Flat 4, Marsh Mansions
Haydown Street
Bloomsbury
London
11th March 1897

Dear Sophia,

It's all right – I'm not going to embarrass you by asking again. I know what your answer is.

I liked fulfilling your task, though. I felt like a knight trying to win a fair lady's favour. Just so you know, my queen, I believe three tasks is traditional. Do not worry – I am not expecting to win the fair lady's hand. Even her handkerchief to wear into battle would be worth it.

Wouldn't you enjoy seeing me abase myself before you? I will do such good for you, I can't tell you. I am so ashamed of those letters I wrote. Please let me atone for my previous failings, if nothing else?

Your noblest knight,

Sebastian

45 Park Lane
Liverpool
13th March 1897

Dear Sophia and Tirzah,

Oh, well done, Sebastian! I wish I could think of a way he could marry you. Life is so unfair sometimes, isn't it?

Of course I like Mr Thompson. He is quite the most interesting and kind man I know. If you mean anything more than that . . . Well! He is much too old for me. (He is twenty-eight; I asked him. Practically old enough to be my father!) (Not really, but you know what I mean.)

I quite agree with you that everyone should be paid . . . but if everyone *were* paid, then there would not be enough money to feed the orphans, or buy them new clothes, or heat their schoolrooms. And while I am all for women's rights, I am not willing to take from those dear babies to pay for them.

I'm afraid I'm actually not sure Mr Thompson likes me at all at the moment . . . so even if I did want to marry him, I don't think he would have me.

It's all down to that account book I stole. I worked on it all evening, and damned confusing it was too. I never had much of a brain for numbers. All those receipts . . . and the lines of credit and debit (I think perhaps I was supposed to have taken the cash box too, now I think of it – there was one on the floor). I got into a terrible tangle. Eventually, Mother took pity on me and straightened it all out (I think).

'What is your Mr Thompson doing giving the accounts to a junior schoolmistress?' she complained. I didn't tell her I'd stolen the account book – she would *not* have been pleased. I just mumbled something about him being ill and me volunteering.

Anyway, it was a terrible long job, and I'm sure we still made some mistakes, even with Mother's help. And it was all for nothing, because Mr Thompson was *furious*.

I had been so pleased about my plan, but it suddenly occurred to me on my bicycle ride into work that perhaps I should have left Mr Thompson a note or something saying where the book and receipts had gone. That actually losing the account book of an important institution like the orphanage was probably a very serious matter indeed. I thought I had better go up to his study straight away, in case he had been worried about it.

Anyway. I went straight up and knocked on the door. I didn't even take off my hat and coat. He was awake and dressed and sitting behind his desk. He jumped up as soon as he saw me.

'Where is my account book?' he said. 'What have you done with it, you wretched girl?'

He didn't look exactly angry – but he didn't look exactly pleased either. He looked rather like Mother trying to tell the children off while also trying not to laugh.

'I've done all your accounts!' I said proudly, opening the bag to show him. 'Well – Mother helped!'

'Phew!' He sat back in his chair. 'Look here, you meddlesome creature, those are confidential documents. If anyone had found out they were missing, I'd have been in terrible trouble.'

'You didn't tell anyone, did you?' I said, suddenly anxious.

'No,' he said. 'Though I should have sent the police after you!'

'And you know I wouldn't have done anything nefarious with them,' I said. I faltered a little. 'Don't you?'

'Yes, I suppose I do,' he said. 'I do trust you – rather against my better judgement. But look here, you rogue. You can't do anything like this again, do you understand? After what happened with the previous super, I've sworn on every holy book in creation to be cleaner than clean – do you hear me?'

I nodded.

'Thank goodness there wasn't anything confidential in this month's accounts,' he said. 'Or I would have to let you go. But I don't think even the trustees could get too upset about you finding out how much we spend on coal and porridge and tea.'

That wasn't quite true. All the wages are in there for one thing, and I'm pretty sure they are confidential. But I thought it best not to mention that.

'You wouldn't mind me looking for a treasurer though, would you?' I said. 'If they were properly appointed and so forth?'

He agreed that that would be quite different. So now I just need to find someone. I decided to run a drawing room meeting to talk about the orphanage and my work there. I asked Mr Thompson to come, but he declined, pleading a trustees meeting. I did very well on my own, though, if I say so myself. Some twenty women came – mostly friends of Mother's and women from church, but a few of my own friends too. I brought photographs of the children and the rooms they live and study in. I showed them some of the work we had been doing with them. I shared a few touching stories of the sorts of homes our children come from. I told them how to adopt a child – and in fact, one woman did say that her sister was looking to adopt! So I may have found one of the children a home of their own! Wouldn't it be wonderful if I had?

They all seemed interested and asked lots of questions. At the end, I told them my plan and asked if they were keen to help out, or knew someone who might be, to speak to me at the end.

I had rather hoped that all twenty of them might volunteer. They did not, of course, but one lady from church said she would be happy to come and teach needlework, and Joan said she would come and listen to the children read. I had to press her quite hard to agree, but I know she is bored now she is home from school, and she is always talking about wanting to do good in the world. The only trouble is, I'm not sure how much of a sticker she is. She dropped out of the church play after three weeks because she wanted to take up golf instead. But it is a start.

Nobody volunteered to do the accounts. I suppose that shouldn't have been a surprise. Mother says treasurer is always the hardest position to fill in any committee, and an orphanage is a much more serious organisation to treasure for than the croquet club.

Poor Mr Thompson! He was back at work today, but he still looked peaky. I think he needs another week in bed at least, but of course I couldn't say that to him. I asked Miss Harrison what is wrong with him, and she said he was born with the bad leg, but that he is just generally run-down and overworked, and that he doesn't sleep well because of the pain from his leg. I would like to send him off to the seaside for a week to recover. But then, I would like to send half the children in the orphanage off to the seaside for a week. I could send him along too to superintend them and kill two birds with one stone. I think you should tell Sebastian he has to find a way for one hundred Liverpool orphans to go to the seaside for a week in August. At the moment we can barely stretch to a day at New Brighton. Shrimping nets, bathing costumes, ices and jellied eels all round are a MUST.

He sounds an absolute dear, I must say.

Your philanthropic friend,

Polly

Bannon House
Abyford
Perthshire
15th March 1897

Dear Sophia and Polly,

Sophia, tell Sebastian he has to find a handsome prince to rescue a poor Scottish maiden locked in a tower. Tell him I demand a young man with half a kingdom, a castle, a noble steed and lots of treasure. He can fall madly in love with me from the photograph you keep ever close to your heart (you *do*, don't you?). And whisk me away on his horse and take me off to be his lady love.

I'll be your treasurer, Polly. How difficult could it be? Can it be done by correspondence?

I am so bored, I would sign up for some worthy committee myself, and you know how unphilanthropic I am. At least it would give me something to do. I expect there are some charitable institutions in Perth. None in our village, though, as far as I can see. There's the parish council, but they wouldn't want me.

Do you know, I spent three hours yesterday lying on my back in my bedroom counting all the roses on the wallpaper. I kept losing count. And yesterday I went into Grandmother's linen cupboard and cut all her best napkins to shreds with the scissors. She won't find out for months; she only uses them at Christmas. I wish she'd find them soon; it would at least mean *something* would happen.

Maybe I will throw myself off a bridge. I am quite a good swimmer; I don't think I would drown. Perhaps then they would send me to an asylum. At least I would have someone to talk to there.

Yours, so bored I could slit my throat,

Tirzah

Wimpole Street
London
18th March 1897

Dear Polly and Tirzah,

I know plenty of rich men, and quite a few of them have mansions by the seaside that lie empty for the winter months. Unfortunately, I can't think of any off the top of my head who would let their houses be overrun by one hundred grubby orphans, my darling, eternally optimistic Polly. You will have to take them all camping instead. Perhaps you could contrive to need rescuing in the night from a spider . . . or for yourself and Mr Thompson to share a tent . . . or . . . What a pity there aren't any bears in Liverpool. Perhaps one might escape from the zoo.

Tirzah, please, please do not jump off a bridge, even in jest. My aunt Emily is a visitor in a lunatic asylum, and she said they are the most boring places in the world. Nothing to do, no books, nowhere to go except exercise in the yard.

I'm sorry this letter is so short. We didn't get in until five a.m. last night, and I have to have my hair done this afternoon in preparation for Lady Ellen's dance. And then Lord St John is going to take me for a ride in his carriage. This is a big deal; he is not the sort of gentleman who regularly takes ladies out for rides. At least, I do not think he is. If I was the sort of girl who liked carriage rides, I'd be in heaven.

Yours ungratefully,

Sophia

Wimpole Street
London
18th March 1897

Dear Louisa,

Is hunting as deathly dull as it sounds? St John goes on and on about it, and I do try to look interested, but my mind just wanders off. Is it like fox and hounds at school? Polly and Tirzah and I always used to get lost at the earliest opportunity and go and lie in the meadow over the school, making daisy chains and gossiping instead.

I hope the answer is yes, because I have a horrible suspicion it is not dull in the slightest but absolutely terrifying. People die hunting, don't they? Like the Squire's son in *Black Beauty*? They go at a fearsome lick, don't they?

I must say, I think your advice to look interested and ask questions was absolutely terrible. St John now thinks I am dying to learn to ride. He is wildly enthusiastic about the whole thing and tells me he went hunting for the first time when he was seven years old, and I should be able to do the same very soon if I want to. I do not want to! I can think of nothing worse! Horses bore me to death. They are smelly and terrifying, and I cannot imagine why people get so excited about them. I really don't want to go hunting, Louisa! Surely it's not compulsory? Would I be terribly frowned upon if I just stayed at home instead?

Your sister-in-a-funk,

Sophia

Grangefield School for Girls
Collingham
Derbyshire
21st March 1897

Dear Sophia,

Oh dear, oh dear, how the mighty have fallen!

Hunting is NOT boring. It is the most thrilling sport in the world. It's the most alive you can possibly feel: it's speed and power and love and – oh! I would have thought you'd be all for it, with your views on the independence of women! Where else is a woman allowed to go galloping about at thirty miles an hour, leaping hedges and so forth? That doesn't happen at a game of croquet, I can tell you.

It isn't as dangerous as all that either, not if you know what you're doing. People do get hurt, of course, but no more than they do playing rugby, I wouldn't think. I never knew anyone who actually died doing it. Not unless you count Tommy Prendergast's uncle, and really, that heart attack could have happened at any time. You can walk round the fences if you don't want to jump over them, though it's rather a bore.

It's all right, I'm teasing. Plenty of people don't hunt, even in the country. Joyce Davidson's mother never did, nor did her sister Marjorie – in fact, that's how I started going, because Joyce said I could ride Marjorie's pony, since no one else was. It's like tennis or whist or painting – some like it, some don't.

Honestly, though, Sophia, surely you know this? Look at Mummy and Daddy. Mummy doesn't know the first thing about painting, but Daddy doesn't care. He shows her his latest masterpiece, and she smiles and says, 'Lovely, darling, I'm so pleased.' And then they carry on talking about politics or the theatre. She's fearfully proud of him, of course, but you can't say she's artistic herself. Poor old Daddy. None of us are, really – except Josie might be I suppose. It's hard to tell when someone is nine.

But my point is, it doesn't matter that Mummy doesn't know one end of a paintbrush from another. That's not why they love each other. Marriage doesn't mean being the same as each other, does it? At least it doesn't for Mummy and Daddy. What does it matter what you think about horses?

Your loving sister,

Louisa

45 Park Lane
Liverpool
21st March 1897

Dear Tirzah and Sophia,

Exciting developments – at least to me. I've found my treasurer!

I got talking to Mrs Henderson at a lecture I went to with Clara and Joan. I've been to ever so many lectures now, and they are interesting. I wonder if any of the lecturers would come and talk to our older children? The thirteen- and fourteen-year-olds would like to know about women's suffrage, I bet. Although we might not get it past the trustees. They are rather inclined to be rather old-fashioned about political reform.

Anyway, so Clara and Joan and I have been going to lectures in an attempt to improve our minds, and afterwards we got talking to Mrs Henderson, who is a friend of Clara and Joan's mother. She was making small talk with me and asked what I did with myself, so I told her about the orphanage and how Joan was coming and listening to the children read. She looked very impressed and said she wished her son were so industrious. He was at university but he had to leave because he got tuberculosis rather badly and had to go to a sanatorium. They cured him, but now he has to wait until September to go back to university, and he is rather dull at home, apparently, with nothing to do.

'But I'm not sure Jonathan would want to come and hear children read their lessons,' she said doubtfully. 'He is more interested in mathematical equations than children, I'm afraid.'

When she said that, I had my brilliant idea. Why shouldn't Jonathan Henderson come and do the accounts for Mr Thompson? I'm sure it would be good for him to get out of the house – or at least his mother thinks it would be good for him, and Mrs Henderson is not someone you want to argue with. He wouldn't need to be paid. And it would tide us over until we found someone permanent.

Mrs Henderson looked a bit doubtful, but she said she would put it to Jonathan. I knew it would probably go nowhere if we left it at that, so I suggested that she and Jonathan come to the orphanage on Saturday to meet Mr Thompson and look around and see what they thought. She looked more enthusiastic about this – people *are* curious about the orphanage, I have discovered. It sounds so much like something out of a novel. And it was agreed.

When we said goodbye, I suddenly thought that I should have checked with Mr Thompson first – what if he had other plans for his Saturday? But when I told him about it, he sort of sighed and said, 'Oh, well, if we get a treasurer out of it, it'll be worth it. But ask me first next time, won't you?'

I said I would do the tour if he wanted, and he could just interview Jonathan at the end. He laughed and said, 'Oh, you'll be coming too, no question of that! But I want to get to know him properly before I hand over the keys to all our money, thank you very much.'

I'm not sure what I was expecting, but whatever it was, it wasn't Jonathan. He was a shy-looking young man, rather tall and thin in a waistcoat with a fob watch and a yellow handkerchief in the pocket. He wasn't a dandy, though – the waistcoat was rather shabby, and his hair needed cutting, and the fob watch was so old it could have belonged to his grandfather.

I felt a little sorry for him, seeing as he'd been bounced into this whole thing by his mother and me, and I wasn't at all sure, as we went round the orphanage, whether he really wanted to be there. He didn't say much, just nodded away as Mr Thompson and I talked. But you could see him taking things in, and the questions he asked were all sensible ones. I think Mr Thompson liked him. And when we went back to Mr Thompson's office, he immediately started asking about the paperwork and what needed doing, and the long and short of it is, he's engaged! For a month's probation, but I think he shall pass, and so does Mr Thompson, I could tell!

At the end of it, Mr Thompson showed us to the door. I said, 'Remember your promise, now,' and he laughed and said, 'Yes, yes!' So I hope he is going to go and have a proper jolly. Heaven knows, he deserves it!

Your gleeful friend,

Polly

P.S. Tirzah, I am sending you a whole stack of *All the Year Rounds*, which Mother was going to throw out. They have got to make for more interesting reading than counting the flowers on your wallpaper.

Bannon House
Abyford
Perthshire
24th March 1897

Dear Polly and Sophia,

I am sorry this letter is so short. I'm having a bad day today. I have a headache, and the world just seems too heavy to hold, somehow. Do you ever feel like that? I suppose you probably don't, you have such busy, interesting lives. I have been in bed all day, thinking about you both, and Liverpool. Weren't the charades fun? Wasn't the theatre glorious? It *was* worth it.

I do think about jumping off bridges sometimes. Not often, but I do. It is three storeys down from the top floor of Grandmother's house. Sometimes when I am very sad, I imagine going up there and opening the attic window and just – jumping.

I think it would be very restful to be dead.

I'm sorry – please don't mind me. It's just that my head is aching so, and Grandmother was so sharp this morning, and I am so tired.

Yours,
Tirzah

Wimpole Street
London
25th March 1897

Dear Tirzah and Polly,

Please, please don't jump out of a window, Tirzah. We love you so much. I am sending you a postal order for one pound. Daddy sent it to me for a new dress, but I have rescued one of Mariah's old dresses instead, so I don't need it. The one pound is emergency money. If you feel like you are going to jump out of a window, send Polly and me a cable instead, and we will . . . Well, I don't know what we'll do, but we'll rescue you, I promise.

In other news, I have thought of a second task for Sebastian. It is not so practical as the first, but if it is done, it will be a jolly good thing – for me and for my aunt Eliza, who I am very grateful to, even if she does drive me to distraction. And it is a *bit* like your suggestion, Tirzah. I'm afraid I am not going to ask him to send you a handsome prince, though. Knowing Sebastian, he would send one of his ridiculous friends, and honestly, I think you would rather stay with your grandmother than end up living with whatever ass would agree to a marriage to help a fellow out. You would end up in a bed-sitting-room in Bloomsbury, living off potted shrimp and rich mixed biscuits and red wine. It would be ridiculous and wonderful for a couple of years, and then completely wretched.

No. My idea is much better. I am going to get Sebastian to persuade Ralph Harrington to ask Mariah to marry him.

Mariah is my older cousin, and I do feel rather sorry for her. It is her third Season, which must really be her last – no one does a fourth Season as an unmarried woman; it would be too shaming.

Mariah is rather a spiky sort of person. She doesn't ever look particularly animated, even when I know she must be. She comes out with the most unexpected things sometimes! But she is a good sort at heart, I think. She is not really the kind of girl who is designed to waltz around a ballroom, batting her fan at people. I sometimes think she would have done better to have been born a man. I can quite see her reading philosophy, or even joining the army and riding off into battle. She has that male directness – none of the feminine charms that are supposed to be so appealing (but I sometimes think are almost shameful).

Anyway, nobody has asked her to marry them, and it looks like nobody will, but there is one gentleman who is interested. His name is Ralph Harrington, and he is an American, of all things – he lives on a ranch in Idaho. He is definitely not aristocracy – I rather think he might be a cowboy – but in any case, he is frightfully rich and has come over to London to visit his aunt, and she is showing him something of the Season.

He is fully thirty-four or -five at least – but he's a good man, very simple and direct, the way you imagine Americans to be. And when he smiles, his whole face comes alive.

He and Mariah get on very well, mostly because they always talk about horses. Can you base a marriage on horses? I don't know, but I am nearly certain she is in love with him. At least, she always looks up when he comes into the room, and she has a smile she only wears when he's there, and if that isn't love, it's close enough for the London Season.

It's not just me who has noticed it either. I heard Aunt Eliza and Uncle Simon discussing it one morning when they thought I was still asleep. (I had come down earlier than usual for breakfast, but of course I froze by the morning room door because I wanted to hear what they were saying.) Uncle Simon was a bit doubtful about sending his elder daughter off to live on a ranch, but Aunt Eliza was quite brisk about the whole thing. She said she would rather a daughter married than a daughter unhappy at home.

The only problem was, Ralph hadn't proposed to her. Of course, young men very often *don't* propose to young ladies they've had a nice time chatting to in a drawing room – after all, I've chatted to heaps of men this Season, and I think they've all had a nice time, and hardly any of them have proposed to me. I don't know, but I decided I couldn't let Mariah's chance of happiness gallop off into the American sunset.

So when Sebastian asked me to dance the waltz at Lady Mary's ball, I told him I'd thought of his second task. He had to persuade Ralph to propose to Mariah. He liked that, of course – his eyes lit up straight away. He sort of glowed all over, and he said, 'Your wish is my command, oh, my fairy princess,' and he bowed low, and I tried not to giggle. I said, 'I should jolly well hope so too, my prince! Off you trot!' And off he trotted.

I shall report back next week with what happens. I know I shouldn't encourage the young fool, but I can't help hoping he succeeds. It would be rather nice for Mariah to get married. And it would be such a snub to Isabelle.

Yours in gleeful optimism,

Princess Sophia of Faerie

Wimpole Street
London
25th March 1897

Dear Louisa,

Were you born an ass or are you just pretending?

It's quite different for Mummy and Daddy. They love each other, for a start. And they like spending time with one another.

I don't have anything in common with St John at all, besides both being a little on the edge of things at the Season: me because I am a poor relation, him because he is shy and awkward and has rather a slipshod and unkempt look about him generally. I like him – which believe me, when you are being sold to the highest bidder at the marriage market, is worth a great deal. But we are not going to make each other laugh like Mummy and Daddy do. I am not ever going to be proud of him the way Mummy is of Daddy – the way it shines out of her whole face when he sells a painting or the press say nice things about his exhibitions. Every time we talk, I have to drag the conversation out of the mud. The only way it possibly manages to go anywhere is to get him started on something that interests him, which is the estate and the hunting and the horses. So there it is. That's all we have to talk about. If I don't talk about hunting, I have nothing. And if I have nothing, so do you.

I suppose it shouldn't matter so much if only it gets us to the altar . . . Except that this is my *life* we're talking about here. I would like to have something in common with the man I'm going to share it with. I can't pretend to feel enthusiastic about shooting things or tearing foxes to pieces, but going for a nice ride in the country sounds like a civilised enough way to spend an afternoon. At least we wouldn't have to talk.

Perhaps if we have children, we could talk about them . . . He would be a good father. That's worth a lot.

You have no idea how lucky you are in Grangefield. Even just little things like the mistresses asking for your opinion and acting like they really care what you say. I remember talking over the future with Polly and Tirzah late at night. Polly was going to be a philanthropist and transform the lives of slum children. Tirzah was going to marry and have six children, a cat, a dog, and for some reason a tortoise.

You'll laugh, but I was going to run a magazine. Running the magazine was my favourite school thing. I was so proud of it, even the dull parts like reviews of school plays and sport fixtures. They used to show it to prospective parents. I always thought I'd go and do something like that. But then Aunt Eliza and Uncle

Simon offered me the Season, and of course that was the end of that idea.

I don't know what you want to do with your life. I've never asked. Are you ambitious at all? When you were a little girl, you wanted to be a coachman, do you remember?

It's all folly, anyway. The Season is nearly over, and I am not saved. So no, I will probably not go out riding to the hunt. But we must have something. It is enough that I am to be miserable; I would prefer not to make him wretched too.

Yours,

Sophia

Grangefield School for Girls
Collingham
Derbyshire
29th March 1897

Dear Sophia,

Sorry. You're right. I'm an ass.
Louisa

P.S. I am grateful, you know. Right now, I just want a life that isn't staying at home keeping house for the Aged Parents. If I could have *anything*, it would be to live in a big house in the country with lots of horses and dogs and a huge garden, and throw parties every year for all the village. Can you just imagine how Daddy would hate it? He hates you going to do the Season too, you know. He and Mummy had a big row after you left. She asked what he thought you should do instead, and if she didn't have enough money to bring us out properly, whose fault was it? She was furious with him. Poor Daddy. She never complains usually, but I know she hates it, having to accept favours from wealthy relations when Daddy's pictures aren't selling. I suppose we shall have to do the same from you when you are married into the aristocracy. What a queer thought.

P.P.S. We had grilled cod with semolina pudding for dinner today. And Miss Williamson gave us a talk about the joys of a married state. Much she knows about it! We are going to have a gymnastics display at the open day. Emma Melgrove is in love with the baker's apprentice in the village. Every time we go into the village, we have to stop and buy a bun, and if he isn't there, she sulks all day.

I suppose school isn't so bad, really, when you consider some of the alternatives. Much love.

45 Park Lane
Liverpool
29th March 1897

Dear Sophia and Tirzah,

Darling Tirzah, you know we love you, don't you? I hope your headache is better and your low mood has lifted. I get disheartened sometimes, but I have never wanted to kill myself. I just get angry and weep, and then I feel better.

How glorious about Sebastian, Sophia. But what on earth are you going to set as your third task? I think it had better be slaying a dragon or you really will have to marry him, you know.

Some drama here too, though nothing so exciting as a proposal. I was eating my lunch on Thursday when Miss Jessop appeared and said that Mr Thompson wanted to see me.

I went up to his office – it was rather strange to see him in his office, I must say. I wonder if his chair hurts him – he looked most uncomfortable in it, with his leg at a funny angle. Anyway, he was smiling, which was nice to see. He has a lovely smile.

'Aha!' he said. 'The chief plotter herself. Your new appointment is excellent – and excessively cheap! You are to be congratulated.'

'I told you so,' I said smugly. 'And you must remember your part of the deal.'

'Indeed, indeed! I keep my promises. Look here – two tickets to *Swan Lake*. You didn't know I liked ballet, did you?'

'No, indeed. Do you?'

'Well – not especially. I confess, I have only been to one ballet in my life, and that was my sister's recital when she was ten years old. But it was this or *Titus Andronicus*, and I spend so long sifting through the wreckage of man's inhumanity to man, I did not want to watch more of it on my day out. But! I do not want to go alone. I am a sociable sort of fellow, when I am well enough, and I would like a companion. And since this whole thing was your idea, I thought I would offer you first refusal.'

He looked at me hopefully. He *was* asking me – it wasn't part of my job. I could have said no if I'd wanted to, and he would have been quite cheerful about it. But I wanted to go. I like Mr Thompson a lot, and I have never seen a ballet before either.

Well, the ballet was on Saturday. Mother was a little worried about me going unchaperoned – even though I explained about Mr Thompson being my superintendent and being ever so old and all the rest of it. At first she wanted to go too – but I begged her not to. I know I'm only just eighteen, but Mr Thompson treats me every bit like a properly grown-up woman, and I didn't want her to remind him that I am not.

She insisted on coming in to talk to him about it, and the upshot was that he agreed to take Betsy along as well. I am not sure who bought her ticket, but Mother said he was perfectly charming and reasonable, and she came out all smiles. So that was all right.

I wasn't entirely pleased with the idea of taking my sister to the ballet with me. Not that Mr Thompson was trying to form an attachment with me or anything like that, but it did make me feel like a child, when I had been trying so hard to feel like a grown-up! But when it came to it, we had a jolly time all the same. Mr Thompson was perfectly charming to Betsy and asked her all about being a nurse and what she thought we should do with the children in the home and how we might improve their general health, which is sadly very poor. Betsy loved it, and even offered to send him over some supplies. She wasn't at all older-sisterish, but perfectly friendly and amenable.

The ballet was . . . incredible. I don't think I've ever seen anything more beautiful in my life. I think Mr Thompson enjoyed it too, although he looked tired by the end – sitting for a long time is not easy for him, and there wasn't much space in the little theatre seats. He would have been better with an aisle seat, but they were all gone.

‘Does your leg hurt?’ I asked him, and he winced a bit.

‘A little,’ he said. ‘But it doesn’t matter. It almost always does, and a trip to the theatre is worth it.’

‘Is it?’ I said, a little anxiously. I didn’t want to make his life harder than it clearly already is.

‘Without doubt,’ he said.

I am not sure he should be in charge of an orphanage; I am sure it is too much for him. Betsy asked him why he was appointed.

‘You are very young for such a job, aren’t you?’ she said. ‘How old are you, anyway?’

I winced a bit at such bluntness, but Mr Thompson didn’t seem to mind.

‘The trustees wanted someone young,’ he said. ‘They wanted someone who could bring a little life and energy to the children. And the truth is, with the rates we pay – those who wanted the job were not those we would want to do it. Faced with a choice between youth or incompetence, they chose youth.’

We stared at him. He smiled.

‘Actually, I was asked to apply,’ he said. ‘My father’s friend is one of the trustees – Mr Olivier.’ We nodded. We knew Mr Olivier. He’s on several other committees with Mother. He’s one of the kinder trustees, the ones who stay to talk to the children when they look round, and sometimes give them a barley sugar. ‘He said – “Get someone who’s young enough to be an idealist and dogged enough to keep going even when the job seems too large to hold,"' Mr Thompson said. 'I do have experience – I helped set up and run a whole school in India. Although that was rather a smaller affair. But we had sixty children by the end, and they all came out knowing more than they did when they went in.'

Betsy asked about his school then, so he told us. He'd been educated in a school for delicate children, apparently – he was ill so often as a child that he could not go away to school with his brothers, and he had been taught at home until he was eleven. Then his mother had heard about this school, and off he'd gone. He says it changed his life. His face sort of came alive when he said it. To have friends – and to be with adults who thought he was worth something and worth teaching. He was worse when he was a child than he is now – he says his mother sent him to a hospital in Manchester for operations on his leg that meant he could walk. 'Until I was nine, I was in an invalid chair,' he said.

When he finished school, he wanted to travel, but his family did not have the money to send him off on a grand tour. The organisation which had set up his school were working with another charity in India which was looking for teachers, so off he went again. 'I hadn't the first idea what I was letting myself in for!' He laughed. 'I was twenty-two, and I arrived, and there was the room, and there was the staff, and we were expected to put together a school from sticking plaster and prayers.'

It sounded like a fantastical undertaking. And rather exciting. I would like to go to India and set up a school from nothing. Except that India seems like such a long way away – I would miss Mother and Father and the children – and the two of you, of course.

All in all, it was a wonderful night, and both Betsy and I were sorry to come home.

'I do like your Mr Thompson,' said Betsy as we were getting changed.

So do I. I like him a lot. I am going to ask Mother to invite him to her next At Home. It will do him good to get out of that stuffy orphanage.

Your balletic friend,

Polly

St Barnabas Preparatory School
Church Lane
Exeter
30th March 1897

My dear Theo,

How goes it in that orphanage of yours? Have you got bored and run off to do something sensible with your life yet? Superintendents are always evil, you know – haven't you read your Dickens? There's nothing dramatic about a superintendent who actually *gives* little Mr Twist some more gruel. And to be honest, anyone serving gruel to orphans in the first place is going to struggle to get a place at the table in Heaven. If you don't start serving them ham and eggs each morning, things will go very badly for you, and don't say I didn't warn you.

More importantly – have you found yourself a wife yet? I have – or at least I will have by the time the summer is out. Her name is Elizabeth, and she is the dearest creature alive (I am obliged by law to say this, but fortunately in Elizabeth's case it happens to be true). Do you think you might be able to come down for the wedding? We don't have a date yet, but probably sometime in August. Even superintendents must get holidays, mustn't they? Do you have a second-in-command? You could make a week of it.

Otherwise life goes well enough for me. The boys are wretched enough, as prep school boys always are, but generally good-hearted. One of them put a frog in my porridge, but he claims it was by accident. Oh, to be of an age when frogs just fall from your pockets into schoolmasters' porridge!

Yours til deth,

Albert

Royal Liverpool Home
for Orphans
Victoria Drive
Liverpool
3rd April 1897

Dear Albert,

Thank you for your letter – and congratulations on your impending nuptials! I would love to come . . . It's been far too long since I've seen your amiable face, and I'd welcome the chance to warn the fair Elizabeth what she's signing up to. But I'm not sure holiday leave is something the trustees thought of when they appointed the superintendent. The teaching staff get school holidays, and I give the orphanage staff a fortnight off in the summer, of course. And the servants all get a half-day once a week. But superintendents must be everywhere and do everything all at once.

It's made more tricky by the fact that I am so often ill. It means I'm permanently behind. I don't have a second-in-command, but Miss Jessop, the school head, has ended up taking on more of the work than I am entirely comfortable with. She is very cheerful about it – they all are – but I do feel sometimes that this place deserves a master with a strength and energy which is entirely beyond me. But then I think of what the previous superintendent did to the orphanage . . . My God! How that man could sleep at night, I don't know. To look at those poor children and take the food out of their mouths . . . I could weep. Yet in a strange way, I should be grateful to him. The staff and children are so relieved to have an honest man to lead them, they forgive me a great deal more than they should.

I do have an assistant now, though – a bright young lad called Jonathan who is on a break from university. He is doing all my accounts for nothing, which seems incredible. One of my young teachers arranged it all for me – a fearsome eighteen-year-old called Polly with a gimlet eye for organisation. I was a little worried when I appointed her as junior schoolmistress that the children might eat her alive. I need not have worried! If I let her, she will reorganise the entire orphanage around me. She is already agitating for me to build a bathhouse and a gymnasium and train all my orphans to march in a parade and heaven knows what!

I took her and her sister to the ballet – I felt I had to, after they found me the assistant. The sister was at the even more-formidable mamma's insistence. Anyway, we had a very enjoyable evening. I had forgotten what it is to do something for the sheer pleasure of it. I had better be careful, though – if I am not, Polly will insist on my throwing a dance for all of Liverpool, and then where would I be?

Yours til deth,

Theo

St Barnabas Preparatory
School
Church Lane
Exeter
7th April 1897

My dear fellow,

I hope you are being careful – both of your health and not to be ensnared by ruthless eighteen-year-olds. Polly sounds like the sort who is difficult to dissuade – once she's reorganised the orphanage, she may decide to move on to reorganising you! Though I suppose an orphanage superintendent is hardly an eligible bachelor.

On the other hand, if you did marry the blighter, she would probably organise the whole thing for you. And she does not sound like the sort to be put off by orphanage life. Maybe you should bow to the inevitable and get on with it.

Elizabeth, I am pleased to say, is twenty-six, so minimal chaperoning required. She has been working as a governess at the home of one of my day scholars, and is the confidential friend of Mrs Tilley, the wife of one of the other masters. She is delighted by the idea of a home of her own, even if it means putting up with

your amiable friend,

Albert

Royal Liverpool Home
for Orphans
Victoria Drive
Liverpool
10th April 1897

Dear Albert,

Heavens! Polly is far too young for an elderly gentleman of twenty-eight like myself. The first time I met her, I half-expected her to be wearing pigtails. But she is not unattractive. She is so enthusiastic about everything – heavens, the enthusiasm of the young! Was I ever like that? I believe I enjoyed watching her enjoy the ballet more than I enjoyed the ballet itself. She has such optimism . . . I do hope working in this place won't destroy that. The heartache that walks through these doors is enough to destroy anyone's faith in humanity.

Still, I think it is good to have a bit of hope. I want so much to improve the lives of the children here, and it is so hard when money and time are in such short supply. I don't mind admitting that my young assistant has made my life much easier. I got to bed before midnight three times this week! And he has given me some space to think about bigger projects. This city is full of charitable organisations – I have set him to researching them to see who might be persuaded to grant us some money. Polly is right that we need a proper bathhouse, with hot running water – at the moment they share one basin of water per dormitory, and by the time it gets to the last children, it is quite cold. I would like to burn the awful wincey uniforms and replace them with something bright and cheerful. Why should orphans wear uniforms, anyway? Don't they face enough hardship without being made to look a guy?

I would like them to have a box each in which they could keep their possessions. Such a simple thing . . . but if you can believe it, before I came, the children were allowed nothing of their own. No toys, no mementos of their families (those that have families – most do or did). Family should be allowed to give them little presents or useful things. We would have to inspect the boxes, of course, to make sure that the children did not hide any contraband. And probably there should be locks, so the children did not steal from each other. That could be tricky with the little ones. The older boys, I am sure, would want to get hold of tobacco or liquor. And perhaps we would have to find some money that they could spend at the shops, so those children who did not have family would not have empty boxes. And then I suppose someone would have to supervise the children and take them to the shops . . . Oh, everything is so complicated when you run an orphanage! And at the moment, I cannot even put my hands on money for one hundred wooden boxes!

It is incredible how little these children have compared to even the poorest Liverpool children. In some ways they are lucky – I know they are lucky. They have three meals a day, a bed of their own, warm clothes, shoes, a toy room filled with gifts from the good burghers of the city. They get to stay in school until they are fourteen (a legal right for all children in our modern Britain, of course, but how many are pulled out early to help with the family!). There are many children in the Liverpool slums who do not have any of those things. And many children in the workhouses and baby farms who do not live past five, or even one. I know we would find it easier to raise money if we did not take on illegitimate children. But when I think of the babies left exposed in the street because the mother has no way to care for them, I cannot bear it.

What those slum children have, of course, is a family, a mother and father and brothers and sisters who love them. What I would like more than anything is the money to place all our children with foster families, not just the babies. I would like the money to support the mothers and aunts and sisters who bring their children here, desperate because they do not have enough to raise them themselves. It costs so much to raise a child in an orphanage, even a penny-pinching sort of institution like ours! How much cheaper and better to give that money directly to the mother and let the child stay with the family. But of course the mother must be made to suffer for her failure to support her child – more so if the baby is illegitimate. She cannot be rewarded. And it is the child who faces the consequences.

Children died in this orphanage. Not so long ago. My children can remember their friends who died. I have them to tea in my sitting room every Thursday, and the older ones talk about them quite matter-of-factly. 'Phyllis who caught diphtheria.' 'Agnes who caught a fever.'

No children have died since I took over. I am determined that none will – at least not if I can prevent it. Of course you cannot prevent everything. I call for the doctor for the slightest temperature or pain – it is an extravagance we can ill afford, but I am haunted by the thought of a little grave with a little occupant who might have been saved.

I know what it is to be excluded, you see. I can remember when my brothers went off to school, and I was left at home. My mother gave me lessons in the schoolroom, and I remember how lonely it was. My brothers learned Latin and Greek while my mother struggled through the textbooks from her own childhood and taught me piano. And compared to the children in my orphanage, I was raised in the very cradle of wealth! I had a family who adored me, every toy I could ever ask for . . . ! And yet, it's funny. I never much minded being ill so often, or having a leg that didn't work. I never knew anything different. But, oh, how I cared about not going to school!

Ah, well. If I can give my children even a little of the world back . . . I will have done something. Though not enough!

Yours,

Theo

St Barnabas Preparatory School
Church Lane
Exeter
15th April 1897

Dear Theo,

I think you should take young Polly out for dinner . . . Encourage her wild schemes! Then perhaps she will persuade the good burghers of Liverpool to build you a bathhouse and send your orphans to the seaside for the week. Consider it an investment!

Yours til deth,
Albert

Royal Liverpool Home
for Orphans
Victoria Drive
Liverpool
18th April 1897

Dear Albert,

If I took young Polly out for dinner, her dear mamma would be so scandalised, she would insist we were married on the spot. And then imagine what she'd do without schoolmarming to fill her days! She would turn us into a model institution, with a floral garden, and all the latest diets and heaven knows what else.

Actually, on reflection, that is not such a shabby idea. How quickly can one book the church?

Yours til deth,

Theo

Wimpole Street
London
19th April 1897

Dear Polly and Tirzah,

You will never believe what has just happened. He's only gone and done it! Mariah will be the future Mrs Ralph Harrington of Idaho, US of A! And it's all down to my ridiculous boy Sebastian.

Mariah is so happy. I don't think I've ever seen her so happy. She makes dry little jokes and she has quite stopped complaining about anything, which is so unlike her as to make me think she has been transformed into a whole new person.

Sebastian is nearly as bad. He's been grinning away like a Cheshire cat since Mariah told us. He has become quite ungovernable. He insists I refer to him as His Royal Highness Prince Sebastian of Fairyland and keeps offering to slay any dragons or tame any unicorns I might have lying around the place.

'But however did you manage it?' I said when I could finally persuade him to stop gloating.

'Oh!' said he. 'The poor fool had no idea the girl was interested in him. Really, your cousin needs to work on her seduction tactics. He thought he was having friendly chats about thoroughbreds and Ascot. When I apprised him of the true situation, he was flattered. I'm not sure he is very intelligent, poor lamb, but a very worthy unimaginative sort nonetheless. I'm sure your cousin will be very happy out there in the wilds of Idaho.'

'But you don't mean to say he only asked her to marry him because you told him she was in love with him?' I asked, marvelling at the simplicity of men. 'It's too *Much Ado About Nothing*!'

'Oh, no! No, it took more than that. He was so worried about her! Would an English lady cope with the privations of the American West? Heavens! Clearly he has never been to an English country house in midwinter. I soon put him straight. Freezing cold, only one flush lavatory per floor, only one plumbed bathroom in the whole place. High ceilings, icy windows, draughts everywhere. A ranch will probably be a paradise compared to Mariah's ancestral home.'

'It's true,' I agreed. Aunt Eliza and Uncle Simon don't live in a stately home – it's more of a small hall – but it is perishingly cold in winter, and everything is tumbledown and about a hundred years old. When we visit, we have baths in hip baths filled by the servants, and they still cook everything on the ancient old range.

'And then he asked if her parents would object?'

Sebastian looked at me sideways, and I raised my eyes at him. He gave me his best smile, warm and a little mischievous. 'Well,' he said. 'That one was more tricky to answer. I didn't exactly like to say that Mariah was fast becoming unmarriageable and that her parents would be delighted to see anyone take her off their hands – it hardly made the poor girl seem like an attractive prospect. Besides, I like Mariah. She doesn't hold a torch to my one and only darling – far too serious – but I would have her above Isabelle without a second's hesitation. I didn't want to make her sound like a millstone, and I know it pleases a man to think his bride a little above his stature in life, as of course Mariah certainly is, in the snobbish sense. So I hemmed and hawed and said that naturally it would be a little unusual, and certainly an aristocrat would be *preferred*, but that marriages between the British upper classes and American millionaires were becoming quite the thing. He laughed a bit at that and said should he get himself a motorcar and a cigar and an apartment in New York, but I told him Mariah would probably prefer an Arab mare. He looked a bit wistful then and said, "Fine girl, that, Fowler," and I knew the thing was in the bag.'

Really, he was quite disgustingly smug, but I did think he'd been very clever about the whole thing. I didn't say so, of course, but I patted him on the head and said, 'All right, my fairytale prince, very nicely done. I shall deign to dance two dances with you on Saturday to show my favour. But don't think you've cracked this nut yet. Lord St John has three houses and a motorcar, you know.'

'Pooh! I laugh in the face of Lord St John!' said Sebastian. 'And I shall claim three dances and one sit-out, two for Mariah and Ralph, and two because I am perfectly charming, and you know it.'

'Oh, you shall, shall you?' said I.

But he did. And very nice they were too.

Your friend from a fairytale,

Sophia

45 Park Lane
Liverpool
21st April 1897

Dear Sophia and Tirzah,

Oh, Sophia! Two tasks down, one to go. Maybe you could challenge him to rewrite the social order of the entire British Isles, so that women may work in professions and all girls are given a London Season free of charge, ballgowns thrown in for nothing. At his present rate, that'll take him about a week.

More excitement here. (I know, it never stops.) I haven't been able to stop thinking about those three boys. What if their father really is still alive? What if he has no idea that his sons are in an orphanage? Even if he is in India, he must have family, mustn't he? Or friends. People do. (I know some people don't, or there wouldn't be any need for orphanages. But most people. I've got so many relations, I lose count.)

What if she's told him they're dead?

I asked Miss Jessop about the stepmother again. Did they get her details? Her address? She said she didn't know. But I kept thinking . . . I know where they keep the records. In the office. All the children's files. I'm allowed to look at the children's files – I'm their teacher. (Well,

I'm Nicholas's teacher). I *write* things in his file. I mean, I could. I haven't.

I thought about just going to the office and asking to see the boys' files. The problem was, I'd promised the children I wouldn't tell Mr Thompson about their stepmother. And if I asked Miss Higham at the office to see the files, she would of course want to know why, and then it would get back to Mr Thompson before the day was done. Miss Higham is a terrible gossip. She wouldn't understand why it had to be kept secret at all, so then I'd have to lie to her and, well, I hate lying. I know it's stupid – but I think of all those years of Miss Clearly telling us that it was a stain on our good name to lie . . . Well, I just hear her, in my head, disapproving of me. And I feel it more since working here. So many of our children have been lied to so many times. I feel like if I make them a promise, I want to keep it. And I didn't see how I could ask about the children's stepmother without either breaking faith with the boys or lying, and I didn't want to do either. So I did something worse. I broke into the records office.

That sounds much more dramatic than it was. It wasn't very dramatic at all. I simply went down into the office after school finished. It was easy. But my heart was pounding the whole time. I knew Miss Jessop and Mr Thompson wouldn't like it if they found out what I'd done, though I hope they would understand the reason.

The children's backgrounds are private, rightly so. They would ask questions I wouldn't be able to answer.

The records office is a grand name for what is basically a storage cupboard. The children's files are kept in several large boxes, going back to the founding of the orphanage in 1835. The current children are sorted alphabetically, fortunately, so I found our boys easily enough. There wasn't much about them, but it did list their parents' names – Maude O'Flannery and Sergeant Eoin O'Flannery.

That was a bit sobering, seeing their names there. I wondered what their mother was like. Nicholas just said she was nice, which could mean anything. What would the poor woman think if she could see her children now?

Their stepmother's name was there too. It said: 'Brought to the orphanage by Mrs Nora O'Flannery, who can no longer care for them.' And there was her address.

I stared at the address. Then, before I could change my mind, I dug in my pocket for my pencil stub and copied it down in my notebook. I wrote the stepmother's name down too. Then I put the files back in their box and left as quickly as I could.

Oh, girls, I did feel so queer! Like I was a thief or something. I know Miss Jessop wouldn't be happy if she knew what I'd done – she is so careful about the children's privacy, she won't let us gossip about them or anything.

I *think* Mr Thompson would understand if he knew *why* – but that, I couldn't tell him!

Which brings me to my next point . . . What on earth am I going to do now?

Your nefarious friend,

Polly

Bannon House
Abyford
Perthshire
23rd April 1897

Dear Sophia and Polly,

I cannot believe you are asking this, Polly! Of course you must go to the stepmother's house and demand to know the truth! Tell her – well, I don't know what you can tell her. That they need to see her husband's death certificate? That the children miss her? (She wouldn't believe that, surely.) That they have a rare medical condition and their wider family must be informed? You must be able to think of something, you are so clever!

And report back immediately! I am desperate to know what happens!

Sophia, I don't want to say I told you so . . . but I told you so. Can I be a bridesmaid when he's slain his dragon? Polly and I would look very fetching in blue, I think.

Tirzah

Wimpole Street
London
25th April 1897

Dear Polly and Tirzah,

Polly, darling, please be careful. It is *so* like Tirzah to cheerfully advise you to waltz straight in, but how will you get there? What sort of street will this woman live on? Please do not go alone, no matter what you do. I quite understand why you don't feel comfortable talking to Mr Thompson about this, but surely you could wait until Michael is home and ask him to go with you? Or your father?

I don't want to sound old-fashioned, but honestly, Polly, between you and Tirzah, I sometimes feel like I'm a thousand years old!

And I am *not* marrying him!

Your geriatric friend,

Sophia

45 Park Lane
Liverpool
27th April 1897

Dear Tirzah and Sophia,

Well, I went. To the boys' house, I mean. I took Sophia's advice, and Michael came with me – he was home for the weekend, which seemed like providence. And I'm glad he did, because it turned out to be quite an adventure.

The children lived on the top floor of a court house – I don't suppose you have court houses in Mayfair and Perthshire, do you? They are tall back-to-back houses, each one room deep, with the washhouse and the privy and the water pump in shared courts. They are cheap housing, mostly, all crammed together as tightly as possible with narrow alleys between them and very little natural light. Nowhere really for children to play, although the alleys and courts are full of children, of course. A lot of the worst housing in Liverpool is court housing, but this house was in an area which is poor but respectable. The windows were clean, and the doors painted, and the houses looked in good repair. Somehow, I thought they might be in one of the slums, but I don't know why – they aren't slum children. It took two omnibuses to get there, even so.

It wasn't much use, though. The door was answered by a little girl about Daragh's age. She said Mrs O'Flannery wasn't there, and 'Mrs Jones lives in her rooms now.' Michael asked if she knew where she'd gone, and she called to her mother.

'Mammy! There's a man here asking about Daragh's mammy!'

It did feel queer, hearing that, that she knew Daragh and the other boys. It felt so strange to imagine them living on this little street, going to ordinary school, playing with the other children.

Anyway, her mammy appeared then, so I explained who we were. She wasn't much use, but she was utterly horrified when she found out where the children were. Apparently the Wicked Stepmother had told her they'd gone to stay with their grandmother, and left the house soon after the children disappeared. She didn't know where Wicked Stepmother had gone to.

She was full of outrage about the stepmother – Mrs Nora O'Flannery, I suppose I must call her. Said she was no better than she ought to be. I'm not *exactly* sure what that meant, but she clearly didn't like her. Said she spent all the money Sergeant O'Flannery sent home on flashy dresses and jewels, and sent the children out begging for their dinner. This must surely be an exaggeration – how many jewels can you really get from a sergeant's pay, especially when he must need some of it to support himself in India? But it's clear that there was no love lost between Mrs O'Flannery and the children.

I asked what had happened to Sergeant O'Flannery, and she said he had died. That was what Nora O'Flannery had told her. She didn't seem too surprised when I explained to her what the boys had told me, said she wouldn't put it past her. I wasn't sure how much of that was just dislike, and neither was Michael. She really hated Nora. And I can't imagine what it would be like to live like that, one family on the top floor, one family on the bottom, one in the middle, one yard and privy and copper between them. It was bad enough sharing a dormitory! (Even with you two, sometimes, and you were angelic dorm-mates compared to some of the people we had to share with in the lower forms, remember?)

I asked if she knew Sergeant O'Flannery's address in India or his regiment. She did know the regiment: it was the 4th Hussars, which was hopeful. I don't know how big regiments are, but they can't be that big, can they? I wonder who is in charge of them and how one finds out where they are?

I asked if she thought he was dead, but she didn't know. I thought perhaps when you lived in a house like that, you would know everything that happened – that the boys would tell her children; that you'd take in the telegram, listen to the wailing, comfort the bereaved. But she said it hadn't been like that. There hadn't been a telegram, and the first she'd heard of it was when Nora said they were moving out because Sergeant O'Flannery was dead, and the boys were going to his mother. I thought that was suspicious, but she said Mrs O'Flannery had 'kept herself to herself.'

'I did think it were a bit queer that there weren't no telegram, but of course, I'm not in the house all the time, I've got the shopping to do, and my washing to deliver.' (She's a washerwoman.) 'Usually, I'd have heard – it's a *grand thing*, a telegram, on a street like this, and folk do talk, but, there! I thought this once, nobody had been watching.'

It didn't seem very likely. The yard and surrounding streets were full of children; boys playing cricket, girls sitting on the steps minding babies. There were grocers' bicycles going past, a man whitewashing a wall, a group of little girls waiting with jugs at the pump. But it was a Saturday, of course. Perhaps weekdays were quieter.

'And she didn't make a big deal of it, that was queer enough. Every day were a drama with her normally! But perhaps she were ashamed of taking the children away. Though heaven knows, it were probably the best thing for the poor little mites. She never did have a maternal bone in her body.'

So that was that. I thought it was very suspicious, and so did Michael, but there didn't seem to be much to be gained by sticking around. I asked if the grandmother was real – if she'd ever seen her – but she sounded a bit doubtful. Said the boys had talked about a grandmother but she'd never seen one. But then they hadn't lived there that long. She didn't know a name or an address. I asked if the stepmother had had any friends in the neighbourhood we might ask, but the woman said she hadn't that she knew of.

'Sour old bag, she was,' she said. 'Sort that would complain about anything if she could. Find silken sheets too slippery and a fur coat too heavy, she would. I wasn't sorry to see her gone, though it did leave me in a pretty pickle, finding another family to cover the rent.'

And that was that. We said our goodbyes and went on our way.

'I think your boys might be right, Poll,' said Michael as we left. 'I don't like the sound of this flit at all.'

And I didn't like it either. Michael suggested we go to the public library and look up the military lists and see if we could find Sergeant O'Flannery in them. I thought that was rather a good idea, only I wasn't sure if non-commissioned officers were in the military lists.

So off we went. Another omnibus. I am glad Mother is sensible about things like omnibuses. I wouldn't be able to work if it wasn't for Mother's sensibleness. I do think some girls live terribly strict lives!

Anyway, so the military lists were no good – nobody below a lieutenant. But Michael had the idea to talk to the librarian, who found us the address of the colonel in charge of the 4th Hussars.

'We can't just write to a colonel!' I said.

But Michael said he would be bound to have aides and things to answer his actual post.

'How else are you going to find him?' he said. So after he'd gone back to Edinburgh, I wrote a letter to Sergeant O'Flannery. Then I put the letter in another envelope and wrote a letter to the colonel, asking him if he knew whether Sergeant O'Flannery was alive or dead, and if he was alive, to pass on this letter to him. That seemed easier than explaining the whole situation, which sounds frankly ridiculous, even to me.

Letters are wonderful things, aren't they? It did seem strange to think of a colonel somewhere in India getting my letter and maybe finding Robert and Daragh and Nicholas's father, and saving the day. I remember when I was eight and decided to write to the Queen. She didn't reply, of course, but I got a lovely letter back from a lady-in-waiting. I couldn't help feeling hopeful as I put the letter in the box. *Something* will come of this. I'm sure.

Your friend from a detective story,

Polly

45 Park Lane
Liverpool
28th April 1897

Dear Colonel Rosewell,

I am trying to find the whereabouts of a member of your regiment, one Sergeant Eoin O'Flannery. I have information which I believe it would be to his advantage to know. I enclose a letter to Sergeant O'Flannery; if possible, please could you forward it to his current address?

If he is dead, please let me know as soon as possible.

This really is very important, I promise you.

Yours faithfully,

Mary Anniston

45 Park Lane
Liverpool
28th April 1897

Dear Sergeant O'Flannery,

I hope you will forgive my presumptuousness in writing to you. Once you know why, I hardly feel you could be anything but grateful, but perhaps I am wrong. If I have misinterpreted everything, I am very sorry. But I do not feel I *can* have misinterpreted things, somehow. I do not think your children would be the children they are if I had.

But I am getting ahead of myself. Apologies.

My name is Mary Anniston and I am an employee of the Royal Liverpool Home for Orphans. Over the last few months, I have been caring for three boys – Daragh, Robert and Nicholas O'Flannery – who I believe are your sons. They tell me that their stepmother, who they describe as neglectful and capricious, left them at the orphanage door. On enquiring, I discovered that this lady had informed the orphanage that you were deceased.

From what the boys have told me of your temperament, I believe that you may be ignorant of your children's fate – if so, I apologise for the natural shock this information will occasion. The boys are well and, frankly, charming. But, naturally, an orphanage is not the home we would wish for them, given an alternative.

Please reply and let me know what arrangement you wish me to make for the boys' well-being. Are there other relations who could care for them? When will you next get leave?

Yours sincerely and anxiously,

Mary Anniston

P.S. If you could spare a moment to write a line to the boys, I know it would be the cause of much delight. They miss you dearly and speak of you with great love and respect.

67 Highcroft Buildings
Manville Way
Glasgow
28th April 1897

Dear Mother,

I regret to inform you that I am in difficulties again. I shall not go into details, but my money is gone, and they say I will be thrown onto the street with nothing if I cannot pay.

I know I am as nothing to you, but if you could only see your way to sending some money – just a little money would do – so your child is not left to starve on the streets, I would be so very grateful. I believe it will be the last time, as I have a good prospect on the horizon: a man who I think will marry me. So you see that it is very important that I can keep the flat. I remain,

your grateful daughter,

Clare

Topmost Bedroom
Witch's Tower
30th April 1897

Dear Grandmother,

I have run away again. Don't worry, not permanently, I don't think. And I haven't gone far this time. I'm going to look for Mamma.

I know she writes to you sometimes when she needs money. I can recognise her hand – the loopy way she does the Ls. I saw there was a new letter on the hall table, so I stole it. It had her address in it, so I am going there now to try to find her.

I know you had your reasons for keeping us apart, but I think it was unimaginably cruel. I remember when I was a little girl at school, how I used to cry at night when everyone was asleep, because I thought she had abandoned me. I bet you never even told her where I was, did you? All those years, I thought she didn't want me, that I'd done something wrong that meant she didn't love me like other girls' mothers love them.

I was so lonely at school, Grandmother. It was a good school – heaven knows how you managed to choose such a good one. But it was hard never getting letters from you or Mamma or anyone. There were other girls there who never got letters – a couple of natural daughters of rich men, or girls whose parents were dead and whose relations had sent them off to school. I wasn't the only child left at school in the long summer holidays, and we made the best of it, those of us who were there. I *was* happy. Heaven knows I wouldn't pay you the compliment of telling you so if I didn't mean it.

But those children didn't have parents or grandparents – not really. (I don't count a natural father who hasn't seen you since you were a baby as a parent.) I did.

I don't know what's going to happen when I find Mamma. Perhaps nothing. Perhaps everything. But I have to try. Please don't come after me. I will let you know that I am safe. I have enough money to get to Glasgow and back from my allowance.

Yours,

Tirzah

FROM: POLLY ANNISTON 45 PARK LANE LIVERPOOL
TO: MICHAEL ANNISTON 4A FERGUSON BUILDINGS JACKSON ST EDINBURGH

TIRZAH MISSING STOP GONE TO GLASGOW TO FIND HER MOTHER STOP HER GRANDMOTHER IN FEARFUL RAGE STOP DO YOU KNOW WHERE SHE IS STOP POLLY

FROM: MICHAEL ANNISTON 4A FERGUSON BUILDINGS JACKSON ST EDINBURGH

TO: POLLY ANNISTON 45 PARK LANE LIVERPOOL

NO IDEA STOP SHE IS VERY UNHAPPY STOP MIGHT SHE HAVE DONE SOMETHING STUPID STOP MICHAEL

45 Park Street
Liverpool
30th April 1897

Dear Michael,

The most awful thing has happened. Tirzah has run away. Her grandmother appeared on our doorstep in an absolute fury. She had our address from Mother's letter to her. She thinks we stole her or helped her or something. Mother had a terrible job convincing her that she wasn't here. She's gone to Glasgow to find her mother.

Michael, you told me when you were here that you and Tirzah were writing. Did she ever tell you she had a mother in Glasgow? Has she been in touch with you at all? She hasn't with us. I thought her mother was dead.

I'm so fearfully worried. Tirzah is a dear, but she just doesn't think. She charges straight off, and anything might have happened to her.

I know it's unlikely, but you aren't so far away. I keep thinking maybe, it she doesn't find her mother, she might go to your flat – she knows your address, at least. If she does, could you wire here at once?

I hope she'll go back to her grandmother's, but she's so miserable there. And I'm sure she doesn't have the money for the rail fare to Liverpool.

I wish I could ask you to go looking for her. But I honestly can't think where you'd begin.

Yours in haste,

Polly

FROM: MICHAEL ANNISTON 4A FERGUSON BUILDINGS JACKSON ST EDINBURGH
TO: POLLY ANNISTON 45 PARK LANE LIVERPOOL

TIRZAH HERE SAFE AND WELL STOP LETTER TO FOLLOW STOP MICHAEL

FROM: MICHAEL ANNISTON 4A FERGUSON BUILDINGS JACKSON ST EDINBURGH
TO: MRS MOIRA LEWIS BANNON HOUSE ABYFORD PERTHSHIRE

TIRZAH HERE SAFE BUT DISTRESSED STOP HAVE FOUND HER SAFE LODGING FOR NIGHT STOP COMING HOME TOMORROW STOP MICHAEL ANNISTON

FROM: MRS LEWIS BANNON HOUSE ABYFORD PERTHSHIRE
TO: MR ANNISTON 4A FERGUSON BUILDINGS JACKSON ST EDINBURGH

HAVE WIRED MONEY FOR EXPENSES STOP PLEASE SEND TIRZAH ON FIRST TRAIN TOMORROW AND WIRE DETAILS STOP MOIRA LEWIS

FROM: MICHAEL ANNISTON 4A FERGUSON BUILDINGS JACKSON ST EDINBURGH
TO: MRS MOIRA LEWIS BANNON HOUSE ABYFORD PERTHSHIRE

TIRZAH ON TRAIN DUE ABYFORD 13.45 STOP MANY THANKS STOP MICHAEL

4A Ferguson Buildings
Jackson Street
Edinburgh
1st May 1897

Dearest Polly,

I cannot imagine how anxious you and Mother must be, but please do not worry – Tirzah is *safe*, she is quite unhurt, only rather upset. I cabled her grandmother and found her a bed for the night and she went back home this morning. I wished I could keep her here with me, but I knew just what her grandmother would say to that and I thought I should do all I could to keep relations between our families as decent as possible. After all . . . But, well! I won't mention that here.

She got here late last night – nearly midnight. Fortunately, McGovern and I were still up – we were coming home from a party in another fellow's rooms. And jolly good thing we were too – we found her in great distress, arguing with the cabbie. She didn't have the money to pay him, of course.

I shall let her tell you the details, but it seems her mother is a dipsomaniac, funding her drinking by such methods as Tirzah did not choose to spell out but can be extrapolated. She is in the habit of applying to Tirzah's grandmother for money when threatened with eviction, and Tirzah got hold of one of these letters and decided to present herself to her motherly bosom – presumably in the hope of finding the love she has been so starved of. Naturally enough, it was not the joyous reunion she had hoped for.

The whole affair took rather longer than she'd anticipated, and she had not enough money to pay for a hotel. She got the train back to Edinburgh but, on trying to change, discovered that she had missed the last train north. In some distress and panic, she remembered that I lived in Edinburgh, and got a hansom to my flat. Thank goodness she had my address with her or I don't know what would have happened to her!

Please do not worry – she is quite unhurt. And I am behaving with all the decorum Mother would expect – and more.

Your loving brother,

Michael

The Dungeon
Abyford
Perthshire
3rd May 1897

Dear Polly and Sophia and Michael,

Well, I am home. And since Michael tells me Grandmother has been bothering you, Polly, I suppose I should tell you what happened. Sophia, I don't suppose you know, but I ran away to find my mother. And I found her and it was awful. I ended up at Michael's flat in Edinburgh, but I couldn't tell him what had happened – I kept crying every time I tried. That's why I've included him in this letter. I think he deserves an explanation, and my heart quails at the thought of writing it all out twice.

I can't remember what I told you about my mother, but I lived with her until I was seven. We were always in wretched houses, and we had to move a lot. I remember one time we had to leave in a great hurry, and I left my doll behind and I wouldn't stop crying, and Mamma bought me a beautiful new one with ringlets. I still have that doll at Grandmother's house.

Mamma was – and is – a dipsomaniac. I didn't know that when I was little, of course. Living with her was very strange. Sometimes she was the sweetest mother imaginable – warm and kind and loving. Sometimes it was like she'd disappeared. She would be sleeping, and I would be sent out to play by one of the men in the house. There were always lots of men in the house. Some of them scared me, but I was never scared when Mamma was there. Sometimes she would be all jagged and angry, and then she'd shout at me, and I'd know to go and hide.

I suppose we were poor, but I don't remember being poor. That was strange too. Sometimes there would be lots of things – beautiful dresses, boxes of chocolates, perfume for Mamma. And then sometimes it would all disappear, and we'd have to run away again. I do remember being cold, and hungry. One awful time we went begging in the street. I remember the way everyone would walk past us and not meet our eyes, and how horrible that felt.

I suppose it wasn't a very good home for a child, but I never knew any different. It had always just been Mamma and me. I adored her, and I know she adored me. She used to tell me so, every day. I used to climb into bed next to her and sleep cuddled up in her arms, and I used to feel so safe and loved. I didn't always feel safe, but I did then.

I don't remember why Grandmother got involved in our life. It was one of our poor periods. We were in the worst lodgings I remember, and I think Mamma was ill. She kept coughing. Maybe Mamma wrote to her, asking for money. Anyway, suddenly Grandmother was there. I remember how angry she was with Mamma. I remember her and Mamma arguing, and Mamma crying. And I remember Grandmother saying, 'Well, if you won't, on your own head be it!'

And then she looked at me and said, 'Do you have a suitcase?'

I did. I showed Grandmother where it was and watched as she packed all my things into it. I was curious about this new person in my life. I wasn't scared of her.

'Are we moving again?' I asked, and Grandmother sort of sniffed and said, 'Them as ask no questions are told no lies.'

So I went back to Mamma, who was lying on her bed. She had the look on her face that she got when she hadn't had anything to drink for too long.

'What's happening?' I said. 'Who's that lady?' And she groaned.

'Listen,' she said. 'Can you go to the Black Bull and ask them – tell them—?'

Grandmother straightened. 'Are you sending your child to buy you liquor?' she asked.

'I do it all the time,' I told Grandmother.

Grandmother looked horrified.

'I am taking this child away!' she said. 'Don't you even want to say goodbye?'

Mamma just moaned. When she got like this, she couldn't think straight or concentrate on anything. I knew that. And I didn't really understand what Grandmother meant when she said she was taking me away. I thought we were going to find a new lodgings for Mamma and me or something. I'd never spent more than an afternoon away from Mamma, so I couldn't really picture a world without her in it. It never occurred to me that this would be the last time I'd see her for years and years and years. Perhaps it didn't occur to Mamma either, because she just moaned and said, 'Oh, go away if you must! Leave me alone!'

So Grandmother tutted and grabbed my hand and said, 'Come along, child!'

And I waved and said, 'Bye-bye, Mamma!'

And that was that. It was ten years before I saw her again.

Grandmother took me home with her, and I stayed in her house for nearly a month. I didn't like it much. I missed my mother, and I kept asking when I was going to see her again. Grandmother mostly ignored me or said unhelpful things like 'In my day, children were seen and not heard' or 'For heaven's sake, child! I don't know! Stop asking me questions, will you?' And then one day, she said I was going to school. I was pleased about this because I liked the idea of school. I didn't know boarding schools existed. I was surprised when Grandmother said we had to buy lots of new things like clean nightdresses and a school trunk. It was Grandmother's maid who told me I was going to a school where you had to sleep.

'But how will Mamma find me?' I said.

She sniffed. 'If you're lucky, you'll never see that mother of yours again!' That was when I realised

Grandmother had stolen me from my mother and I wasn't going back.

I liked school, though. Maybe it was because the teachers were kind, unlike Grandmother, who always looked bewildered by me, like she didn't know what to do with a little girl. I suppose she didn't. Mamma and Aunt Lucy were raised by nannies. I liked how everything was the same at school – you always knew when you were going to get fed and what was going to happen next. It made me feel safe. I liked the pretty dresses Grandmother had bought me, and I liked dancing and music and gymnastics. And I liked Miss Flint, who taught singing. There were only a few little girls like me there – I wasn't quite the youngest, but nearly – and the older girls used to mother us a bit. I was used to living in a noisy, busy place – there were always people in Mamma's flats and tenements – so I liked all the drama of a school too. I hated Grandmother's house for being so quiet – I was always being scolded for running, or picking things up that I wasn't supposed to touch, or asking questions.

At first I hated Grandmother for stealing me from Mamma. But after a while I started to hate Mamma too. Why had she never come to look for me? She knew where Grandmother lived. Why didn't she come swooping in on a train and rescue me? That's what I'd do if someone stole a child of mine. I wouldn't stop fighting until I got her back.

I'm sorry. This is quite the longest letter I ever wrote. I didn't mean to put all that down. I haven't even got to what happened on Saturday.

So, I never told you, but last December, I found a letter from my mother asking for money. I wrote back, but the letter was returned to me, saying she'd been evicted for not paying the rent. So I thought that was that. But I kept looking at the hall table, and last week, I found another letter from her, saying the same thing.

And I just thought . . . I wanted to see her again. I wanted to know what really happened when I was taken away. Did she ask Grandmother to look after me? Did she try to find me? I suppose I thought she might be my second nut . . . though I didn't really think she would be a hiding place. But she might be.

It wasn't very difficult to get there. I took your money, Sophia, and what was left of my dress allowance. I told Grandmother I was going into town to do some shopping. And then I just got on a train to Glasgow instead.

I didn't know where Mamma's flat was, so I had to take a hansom. The address was in a big tenement building, which was a bit of a shock. I spent half my childhood in flats in buildings like that. I'd forgotten. It gave me a jolt, seeing the building, with the washing hanging out of the windows, and children playing in the gutters, and women standing gossiping on the corners. They all stared at me, and I nearly turned around and went straight back to the station. But I'd left Grandmother a letter, and she would have found it by then. And I couldn't bear to admit that I'd failed.

Her flat was very easy to find. I knocked on the door, and nobody answered for ages, and then . . .

There she was.

For a moment, I didn't recognise her. She was horribly skinny – sort of typhoid-victim skinny. And she had these awful sunken eyes, all raw and red around the edges. She had chilblains on her fingers and long, wild-looking hair. I was almost frightened of her. No, I *was* frightened. But I did know it was her, once I'd looked at her. And she knew it was me. You wouldn't think she would, after so long, but she did. She grabbed my arms and she said, 'Tirzah! Oh, Lord! Tirzah!' And she began to cry. Great, rasping sobs.

She put her arms around me, and I found myself crying too. I didn't expect to. I mean, I suppose I had expected to when I'd imagined a wonderful reunion. But this mother wasn't the mother I'd imagined. Perhaps that's what I was crying about. Or perhaps it was just everything, the whole last ten years, and all these months at home with Grandmother.

She pulled me into her flat. It was dark and filthy and furnished with the old hodgepodge of furniture you get in rented places. I'd lived in lots of places like this, I remembered.

'Oh, Tirzah! I knew I would see you again one day!' she babbled. 'I just knew it! That old witch couldn't keep us apart! Oh, my darling, you've come back to me!'

She was drunk.

I drew back a little, but she pulled me forward.

'Oh, where have you been? You must tell me everything – I insist! Absolutely everything!'

I didn't know what drunk was when I was a child – though heaven knows, my mother was intoxicated often enough. But I know now. I've seen the men at the Durham Ox drunk, and I saw those men in the street in Liverpool the Christmas before last. I know what drunk is, and when I saw my mother now, a lot of my childhood started to make a strange, sad sort of sense.

'Grandmother sent me to school,' I said. 'I've finished now.'

'Oh, how horrid!' she said. 'I hated that woman. I suppose you hate her too, don't you? But now you have come back to me, my darling.'

It was awful. I think part of me must have known it would be – I always knew she could have found me if she'd really wanted to. And of course she was really quite a stranger to me. We didn't know each other at all. I *do* remember her, but the mother I remembered was quite different to this one – much bigger, and much less of a *person*. (I suppose mothers and fathers are never really people to children, are they?) When I was a child,

I never thought about whether my mother was a good person or a foolish one or the sort of person one wanted as a mother. She was just my mother, you know? But standing here now with her there across from me, I knew why my grandmother had taken me away. And – oh, it's awful, but it's true! – I wasn't sorry she had.

She pulled me onto the sofa – it was a horrible sofa, with a sticky black stain on the back – and kept gabbling away about how dreadful my grandmother was and how pleased she was to see me. She started to cry again, and so did I. I couldn't help it. She seemed to like that; she hugged me and babbled on about how much she loved me and how much she missed me.

'I wrote and wrote and begged her to give you back, but she never did!' she cried. 'She wouldn't! That bitch – I hate her, don't you? Don't you hate her?'

I didn't know what to say. I do hate my grandmother . . . Except, looking around this filthy room, I found the words stuck in my throat rather. So I muttered something and changed the subject at once, asking how she was, and what she had been doing and all those things.

'Oh! I am not doing so badly now. Only it is so hard, is it not, with the price of everything. But now that *you* are here, all will be different – we can find some work for you, and you can help and . . .'

She wanted me to stay.

She thought I was there for good.

'Oh, no!' I said. 'Oh, Mamma, I can't stay! I have to be back on my train today. I just came – I just wanted to see you – I didn't mean to stay for ever!'

That wasn't true. I had thought I might be able to stay with her. But now of course that was impossible.

Anyway, it was dreadful. At first, she pretended she was all right with me going, but it was clear that she wasn't – she cried and wailed and said I was abandoning her and I didn't love her. I didn't know how to respond to that one. I mean, I loved her very much when I was seven years old, but I hadn't seen her in over ten years. This woman was a stranger to me. Can you love a stranger? I don't know. And I was too overwhelmed to answer.

At last, I managed to leave, after many tears and exhortations to write and not to forget her. I didn't have much money left, but I had just enough for a hansom to the station. I caught the train to Edinburgh and sat in the corner of the carriage, looking out of the window and trying not to think. I knew Grandmother would be furious when I got home, but I didn't care. I just wanted to be somewhere that was safe and warm and clean. It frightened me to think that I'd lived like that as a child. Though I don't think it was as bad then. It *mustn't* have been, must it? Surely I would have remembered? I remember being happy living with Mamma. But the more I thought, the more I began to remember other things, things I'd put out of my head. The nights when she went out and left me there on my own. The times when there wasn't food. Some of the men who used to come to our rooms, and how frightened I was of them. I don't think she was such a drunkard as she is now. But that doesn't mean it was a safe place for a child to be.

I wondered what would have happened to me if I'd stayed there. It was such a strange thought. I could not really hold it.

I got off the train at Edinburgh and asked a guard when the next train home was. He told me it had already gone. I was stranded in Edinburgh. I had no money. And nowhere to go.

I began to panic.

What could I do? Were there charities that could help? How would I even find them? Could I sleep in the waiting room? Surely it wouldn't be open all night? Would it? Should I go back to my mother? But no, I didn't even have the money for that. Perhaps I could go to a hotel and ask my grandmother to wire me the money. But knowing her, she would probably abandon me there to teach me a lesson.

I'm not ashamed to say, I sat on a bench and wept. It had been a horrible day.

In the end, I did the only thing I could think of to do. I went and knocked on Michael's door. I know it is not very seemly for a young woman to appear on the doorstep of a young man she barely knows, but these were desperate times. If I'm honest, I think I was always going to end up there. Michael and I have been writing to each other, you know. Did I tell you that? Well, we have.

I did not know how far away he lived, but I hailed a hansom anyway and just hoped he would be there and able to pay. I was fearfully nervous – I knew he must think me an awful fool. But I couldn't see what else to do.

So I went, and it was all right. He was there, and he paid for the cab, and he found me somewhere to stay, and really he was very lovely (you were, you know, Michael. I am very grateful), and I will tell you girls all about it properly at another time, but right now I am so tired, I must stop. This letter has taken me three whole days to finish.

Michael, don't imagine you'll be included in all my letters to the girls, but I had so much to say in this one, I couldn't bear the thought of writing it out again. When you've read it, please send it to Polly, and she will pass it on to Sophia when she's finished. It is rather a strange scheme, but it does work.

I hope you haven't been very worried about me. I love you all.

Your sad and weary friend,

Tirzah

45 Park Lane
Liverpool
6th May 1897

Dear Tirzah,

I am sending you some toffee and a rather distinguished stuffed bear called Harold. The toffee was made by the children (our children, not the ones at the orphanage), so I can't promise it's very hygienic, but it tastes all right.

The bear was mine when I was small. I know he's rather an odd present, but he is very comforting to cuddle. I wanted to send him to remind you that even if you don't have the mother you might have wanted, you do have Sophia and me. I hope your grandmother is not too cross, and that Michael behaved himself. He is very fond of you, you know.

I love you so much, Tirzah. I'm so sorry about your mother.

Polly

Wimpole Street
London
7th May 1897

Dear Tirzah,

So much love, my darling. I'm so sorry. You could have told us about your mother before, you know. We wouldn't have minded.

And it isn't your fault. It was never your fault. You didn't do anything wrong.

I am sending you some *very* expensive scent to cheer you up. It was my Christmas present from Aunt Eliza and Uncle Simon, but it makes me sneeze, so I am passing it on to you.

You can't leave the story there, though! What about the dashing young doctor who rescued you from the streets? Honestly, it's like something out of the serial in *Girl's Own*!

Your loving friend,
Sophia

P.S. He couldn't take his eyes off you at Polly's party. It wasn't just me who thought so. Your auntie Sophia approves.

Bannon House
Abyford
Perthshire
8th May 1897

Dear Polly and Sophia,

Thank you so much for your kind messages, and for the presents, Polly. I started crying again when I saw Harold. I do remember you having him when we were at school and how comforting he was to hold. I think he remembers me as well. He is sitting on my writing desk now, watching me with the most *knowing* expression. He sends his love and says he likes his new home, but he is not sure about Dinah, the kitchen cat. And tell the children the toffee is excellent.

Michael . . . well. I know he is your brother, Polly, but Michael was marvellous. It turns out he lives in a tenement flat on the fourth floor – I couldn't pay the cab driver, and he didn't want to let me go up and borrow the money from Michael. He wanted me to leave my bag there as security, but I was terrified he would drive off with it and then I would have nothing. I suppose I should have just climbed down and walked off anyway – he couldn't exactly stop me, and it wasn't as though I had the money to give him – but I do so hate to be thought badly of. I kept saying, 'My friend lives up there – if you'll just let me go and ask him, I can be right down.'

And he kept shaking his head and saying, 'Aye, but I've only your word for that, haven't I?'

Fortunately, just as I was nearly starting to cry again – I have cried so much in the last week, I think I must have run dry – Michael himself appeared, with McGovern, the fellow he lodges with. He was wonderful – he saw in an instant what needed to be done, paid the cabbie, and took me straight upstairs. Have you been in their flat, Polly? It was the most wonderful sort of chaos – coffee cups and plates and whisky bottles and envelopes and newspapers and handbills absolutely everywhere. There was a skull on the coffee table acting as a candlestick (I thought it was a real one at first, but it turned out to be china). And toy soldiers on manoeuvres on the mantelpiece. There was also a hole in the wall that you're not to tell your mother about – apparently they had a party that went a bit wrong.

Anyway, Michael and McGovern were very sweet to me. Michael made me a cup of coffee with brandy in it – for shock, you know. I'm not sure how much sense I made, but they seemed to know about me being missing already. Michael said he would cable my grandmother, which made me sob again, but I knew of course that it was the right thing to do. McGovern said I could sleep on the sofa (actually, he said Michael could sleep on the sofa and I could have Michael's bed), but Michael said that wouldn't do at all and that he would find me somewhere more respectable to sleep. McGovern was inclined to laugh about this rather, but Michael said, 'Hush! Her grandmother is very strict. If she were to think . . . !' And that shut him up at once.

They weren't sure where to put me, and they suggested various hotels and guest houses, then Michael said, 'Ah! I have it! Mrs Wade!' and McGovern said, 'The very place!'

Mrs Wade turned out to be the lady who lives in the flat below them. She takes in lodgers, only her current lodger had left last week, so the room was free. She was an absolute darling. McGovern went downstairs to explain the situation to her, and when I followed him down – still red-faced and weepy – she was just wonderful.

'Not to worry, hen,' she said. 'You hop into bed, nice and warm, and it'll all come out in the wash.'

I think if I had to be adopted by a grandmother, I would like her to be Mrs Wade. She put clean sheets on the bed and a hot-water bottle between them. I thought I wouldn't be able to sleep a wink, but I was so tired that I can't even remember closing my eyes.

When I woke up, everything was still just as strange and lovely. Mrs Wade brought me hot tea and buttered eggs and toast in bed, as though I were ill and needed feeding up. I had a bath in a tin bath in the kitchen, by the range. (She shut the door, so I was private, but it was still very strange to be sitting there surrounded by all her crockery and pots and pans and things!) And then when I was dressed, Michael came downstairs to tell me that my grandmother had wired the money for my train fare, and I was to take the next train home. (It was supposed to be the first one, but we missed that. Michael doesn't do early mornings, except when he has to.)

'Is she fearfully angry?' I said, and Michael said, 'It's hard to tell from a telegram.'

I looked down then – I felt so cared for and also so lost and empty, and . . . like I'd been picked up and put aside from my real life, if that makes sense. There's the ordinary Tirzah, who went to school, and writes letters, and annoys Grandmother, and then there was this one, who sat in medical students' flats, and drank Mrs Wade's tea, and was the daughter of a ruined dipsomaniac. I just felt washed out and empty and utterly alone. I know I have you girls, and I'm really very grateful, but you're not the same thing as a family.

'I suppose you must think me ridiculous,' I said. I wasn't fishing . . . All right, perhaps I was, a little. I have so few people who care about me – I wanted to know if Michael was one of them.

'A little,' he said. I looked up quickly at that. 'But I also think you're brave. And clever. And magnificent.'

He said it with such admiration in his voice . . . like he really meant it. I was astonished. Nobody has ever called me magnificent before. I carried the way he said it – 'Magnificent!' – folded close to my heart all the way home.

Your sadder but still foolish friend,

Tirzah

Wimpole Street
London
10th May 1897

Dear Tirzah and Polly,

Well, Tirzah, it looks like you are going to find a husband before me. I don't know why I'm surprised. You and Michael will make a very nice match indeed. Your house will always be untidy, your bills will never be paid on time, there will be half-dissected kidneys left abandoned in the scullery, and all the beggars in the parish will get their tonsils taken out for nothing. But your house will be full of singing and laughter, and young men coming over to eat fish and chips and drink beer, and Michael will wear that soppy expression he wore when you started singing at Polly's birthday for the rest of his life. I should think you'll be very happy together.

As for me, I have put it off for long enough, but I have decided. I am going to arrange a time and a place for Lord St John to propose to me, and when he does so, I shall accept him.

You never say anything, Polly, but you don't have to – I know you think it is wicked to do what I am doing. Sometimes I think I agree with you. But if I do not do it,

I am asking Louisa and Becky and Ethel and Josephine to do it in my stead. And surely that is a worse wickedness?

Yours pragmatically,

Sophia

67 Highcroft Buildings
Manville Way
Glasgow
10th May 1897

My darling Tirzah!

Oh, how wonderful it was to see you again! You don't know how many nights I have sobbed over you. I knew you would come back to me, my darling.

Is your grandmother treating you well? I could weep when I think of her sending you away to that horrid school! You must come back and live with me, my darling. We could be so happy together! Just like we used to be! It was so cruel of fate to tear us apart like that, but now we are together, we will never let it happen again, will we?

There is only one bed in this flat, but I think I shall be moving out soon – the landlady is so horrid! I had thought perhaps I was going to be married . . . but it was not to be. It does not signify. I shall make sure there are two beds in my next place, one for me, and one for my beautiful daughter. It gave me quite a start to see you, my dear, so tall and so distinguished! You must marry a rich man and keep us both – I insist upon it! I'll wager your grandmother does not let you go to dances, does she? I should not be so cruel. A young girl needs male society.

Write soon, my darling, and tell me all your news. And if you could intercede on my behalf to your grandmother about the small matter of the money I wrote to her about, I should be so grateful. I hate to mention it, my dear, but it really is very necessary right now.

Yours in anticipation,

Mamma

Bannon House
Abyford
Perthshire
12th May 1897

Dear Mamma,

Thank you for your letter. How are you? I am well. I am glad we met, and I hope we can keep in touch.

I'm sorry, but I do not think I will be able to come and live with you right now. I hope you understand that when we have been reacquainted for such a little time, it would be too sudden to uproot myself again.

I don't know what I think about Grandmother. I do wish she could have been a mother to me. I wish she had let me see you, and let you write me letters. And I wish she had taken more of an interest in what I was doing. But I loved my school. I really did. I would have been miserable cooped up in this stuffy old house.

I hope you are well and have found a new place to live. I mentioned your predicament to Grandmother, and she sort of harrumphed and said something not very kind. So I don't know if you will be getting any money or not. I'm sorry.

My friend Mr Anniston says there are some very good temperance charities now helping people to stop drinking. He gave me a pamphlet all about it, so I am putting it in the letter for you to read. But whatever you do, I remain,

your loving daughter,

Tirzah

P.S. Please write back.

Wimpole Street
London
12th May 1897

Dear Sebastian,

I think you should know that I'm going to accept Lord St John's proposal. He hasn't actually proposed yet. But he's making all the right noises. I expect it'll happen any day.

I'm putting this in a letter because I can't bear to tell you to your face. I know there is a part of you that has hoped I might change my mind – there is a part of me that has hoped so too, if I'm honest. I never really, truly believed I would marry him. The Season feels so unreal, like such a game. (Does it feel like that to you, who has grown up with it, or just to me coming from my funny little house in Derby?) I thought my fairy godmother would swoop in and save me. Isn't that strange? If anything, it's an anti-godmother I need. I've been to so many balls. But what I really wanted was to sit at home by the fireside, with you.

I am crying again. I never cry. Please don't cry too. You will be all right. You are good and kind, you will find another girl to love without much trouble. I do hope you will be happy. This would be so much easier if I thought you might be happy. Please be happy, for me.

Enough. I love you. I never said it before, did I? But it's true.

Goodbye,

Sophia

45 Park Lane
Liverpool
14th May 1897

Dear Tirzah and Sophia,

Sophia, I don't think you're wicked – I could never think that. But I do think it is wrong to marry for money, yes. I don't think it's fair on Lord St John – it's like selling him a dog with a false pedigree somehow. And I don't think it's fair on you either.

I can't explain what I mean very well – but it's like how suicide is still a crime, even though you're only murdering yourself. Murdering yourself is still a wrong thing to do. You matter as much as everyone else, and so does your happiness, and even though I know you've chosen this, you didn't really have much choice in the matter, did you? So no, I don't think you're wicked, but I do think the system that requires you to sell yourself is wicked, and I'm sorry to say it, but I am a little angry at your parents for asking you to do so. Only because I love you so much, and I hate to think of you being unhappy! I know this is quite usual amongst the upper classes . . . but I am just a normal girl from Liverpool, and I cannot understand it at all.

I'm sorry. Please, darling Sophia, I hope I haven't offended you. I think you are truly marvellous, and my friendship with you and Tirzah is one of the things I hold most dear in all the world.

Tirzah, I did know you were writing to Michael – I hope you don't mind, but he asked me for your address, and of course I asked him if you had replied. I should warn you as his sister that he is incorrigibly messy, occasionally lazy and flippant, and that last year he got horribly drunk at a university party and was locked out of his flat and had to spend the night asleep on a park bench.

However, he is also warm-hearted, loyal, kind, and a good friend in a tight situation. All in all, I approve.

Much love to you both,

Polly

Bannon House
Abyford
Perthshire
16th May 1897

Dear Michael and Polly and Sophia,

Strange times here! I have had an Actual Conversation with Grandmother! I know! In which we actually talked about things like adults. I couldn't believe it either.

I was sitting with her after lunch, and she asked what I thought of my mother. I said I thought she looked ill, and she made a sort of 'Ha!' noise. 'Can you see why I took you away, my girl?' she said.

I did, but I wanted her to tell me what had happened, in her own words, so I asked her. I didn't really expect her to answer, but she did. She said that my mother had written begging for money. She was ill, she said, and couldn't look after her little girl. I am sure my mother wrote this to speed her enquiry, not out of any presentiment of what Grandmother would do. So Grandmother had taken the train to Glasgow and, on seeing the circumstances of our life, decided that my mother was an unfit parent and removed me straight away.

'What did my mother do?' I asked. 'When she found out what you'd done?'

‘Oh, she sent me all sorts of wailing letters. Even showed up at the house once, screaming and crying. I told her very plain: if she was willing to live like a respectable woman, and to put aside her drinking, I would be happy to give her a small allowance, enough to provide a decent home for the two of you. Not here, naturally, but a small cottage somewhere, where she could give out that she was a respectable widow. Or perhaps we could find her some work, as a housekeeper or suchlike – a decent job where she could have you with her.’

‘What did she say?’ I was fascinated. I don’t know why, but it had never occurred to me that my grandmother would have given my mother a way to get me back. I had always thought of her as the ogre in our story. The thief. The villain. Though I admit the idea of my mother as a housekeeper was rather an unlikely one. But a little cottage, just the two of us – it seemed too like a dream to be true.

‘Oh, she ranted and raved. Said I had no right to take her daughter, and she would call the police on me. She never did. And she clearly did not care tuppence for you, since she was not willing to do so small a thing to reclaim you.’

I do not agree with Grandmother about this. Giving up drinking would not be a small thing for my mother. But I was shaken to hear that she could have had me back and did not. Perhaps the cottage felt to her like it did to me – something out of a fairytale, too intangible to be real. Or perhaps she was simply too despairing. I don't know. I would like to ask her. Perhaps one day I will.

'Do you often give her money?' I said.

Grandmother shrugged. 'Perhaps two or three times a year, she sends me another letter. I sometimes pay her creditors, but I do not give her money to spend on drink. Though I suppose it amounts to much of the same thing.'

I was silent. I did not like this version of my mother. I don't know exactly how I'd thought of her over the years – sometimes she was the hero of the story. Sometimes she was the villain. Sometimes it was my fault she'd never turned up. I used to read stories about orphans who were dumped on people who didn't want them. And usually the orphan would be so sweet and winning – all blond curls and affecting lisp, you know – that the person would decide they loved them anyway. I used to hate those stories. Because why hadn't that happened to me? Why did my mother not want me, and why did my grandmother not want me? What had I – a little thing of seven – done that was so bad?

I didn't say any of this to Grandmother, of course.

'Is that why you lost touch?' I asked instead. 'Because of her drinking?'

Grandmother sniffed.

'No, that was her doing. She formed an alliance with a most unsuitable gentleman she met at a dance—'

'My father?'

For some reason, I had never thought much about my father. When I was little, I didn't know that everyone has a father. When I realised that I must have one somewhere, I thought perhaps he was one of the many men who came and went in my mother's life. It had never occurred to me that my grandmother might know who he was.

But she nodded.

'Just so. She was a wild girl. We had taken a house in Edinburgh, your grandfather was alive then, and she formed an attachment to a devilish gentleman with a wife of his own – a sickly sort of girl too ill to attend dances, but a wife nonetheless. We thought it was foolishness at the time, but naturally we did not expect anything to come of it. Then, when his regiment was moved away, we discovered that you were expected. I tried to make arrangements, but she would have none of it. She took some jewellery from the house and ran after the regiment. What she expected to happen, I do not know – that he would support her, perhaps? But of course he did not. How could he? She found some other officer to keep her, and when he threw her off, I suppose she found another. I don't know. I wrote to the regiment, but they said she wasn't their concern – and she only nineteen! They should have been ashamed of themselves!

In any case, I swore the same thing should not happen to you or Lucy. We took Lucy away from Edinburgh, and she lived a quiet life at home with us. You shall do the same.'

I didn't know what to say to that. It was so desperately sad. Aunt Lucy was three years younger than mother, I knew. And she died two years ago. If Mamma was nineteen when I was born, Aunt Lucy couldn't have been older than thirty-one when she died. I know that sounds fearfully old, but it isn't really. I wondered if she had liked living at home with Grandmother. I didn't see how she possibly could.

'Grandmother,' I said carefully. It was so rare to see her in this confidential mood, I did not want to ruin it. 'I do like Mr Anniston very much.'

Grandmother looked rather surprised by this sudden sideways leap.

'He is a medical student, you know,' I said cunningly. Grandmother loves doctors.

She looked even more surprised, then she gave a dry, throaty sort of laugh.

'Gracious, child!' she said. 'You have told me that five times already!'

'Well, he is,' I said. 'And he's very respectable. He wouldn't let me sleep in his flat, though I wouldn't have minded. He was very kind and helpful. And—'

'And he is a very eligible young man,' said Grandmother.

I gawped at her.

'Good heavens, child!' she said. 'I am not stupid! I hope you aren't intending to elope with him, are you?'

I would if it came to that, but I didn't say so.

'He hasn't even asked me to marry him,' I said. 'He's a student . . . so even if we did get engaged, we couldn't marry for years and years. But he's a good man, Grandmother.'

Grandmother snorted.

'Too good for you!' she said, but I didn't mind. She's right, anyway.

She changed the subject then, but it didn't matter. I think I've won. I'm not sure how, but I have.

Love to you all,

Tirzah

Flat 4A Ferguson
Buildings
Jackson Street
Edinburgh
17th May 1897

Dear Polly,

I am sending you the enclosed as requested. I expect you will be very shocked when you see what Tirzah has written about me. I know it's very forward of her, but it did make me laugh.

I have never asked Tirzah to marry me, or been anything other than respectful towards her . . . but I think one day I may want to. Tell me, is that an absurd idea? You know her better than I do. I think she's a darling girl. But she's very young, of course . . .

Would I be making a terrible mistake if I asked her to be my wife?

Your loving brother,

Michael

Flat 4, Marsh Mansions
Haydown Street
Bloomsbury
London
17th May 1897

Dear Sophia,

I hope you don't think me rude for not replying before. I have been trying and trying not to write this letter, because I know your mind is made up and I do not ever want to hurt you. But I cannot leave it unsaid. I know if I did, I would regret it for the rest of my life. That isn't hyperbole. It's the plain truth.

Please don't marry him. Does your father really want you to make yourself miserable for those sisters of yours? I can't believe it. And why should you be the one who throws yourself away for their happiness? Why shouldn't they marry rich? You didn't choose to have five penniless daughters – your parents did. Why are they therefore your responsibility?

I know what your answer is going to be – because you are the one who has been gifted a Season, and therefore you are the one with the best chance of success. But, Sophia, I have seen all the work you do for your aunt. The fetching and carrying, the letter writing, the reading aloud, the bags carried and the visitors declined and the errands run. The work you do for your cousins, distracting the men your aunt doesn't want them to dance with, or directing the men she wants towards them. Don't think I haven't noticed. Mariah will be married this summer, but unless something unexpected happens, Isabelle will have another Season, won't she? Can't Louisa take your place?

And if she can't . . . why do you all need to marry aristocrats anyway? Your parents are happy, aren't they? I may not be able to stretch to a Season, but I can certainly introduce your sisters to marriageable types, if that's what's worrying you. I am a sociable fellow, as you know. We could invite them here in the hols, they could fetch your books for you and wind your wool, and we could take them out and about and introduce them to the more attractive half of my family's address book. Why not?

Sophia, your dutifulness is very becoming . . . but you are one of your father's daughters as well. Don't you deserve to be happy too?

Your one and only,

Sebastian

45 Park Lane
Liverpool
19th May 1897

Dear Michael,

Well, well! I suppose I shouldn't exactly be surprised . . . Indeed, it would be more surprising if you were writing to her *without* such intentions. Nonetheless, I am glad to hear it.

As to Tirzah, I think she is one of the dearest girls I know. She is sweet, funny, lively, and very, very loyal. If she decides she likes you, she will be your friend for life. I have reason to know it.

As to her faults? Well, she is very young for her age – too young perhaps to be engaged, certainly too young to marry. She is rather flighty. She has no ability to stick at anything difficult – you would have to look after her a great deal, I think. She can be foolish and reckless. She would be a very loving mother, but she has no notion of what a normal childhood is like – I think if you want children, you should send her to live with Mother for a year, to see how children should be raised. She is half a child herself – I know she's only seven months younger than me, but I think Sophia and I are ten years older than her in some ways. But in other, sadder, ways she's much older than we are.

Sophia and I have been her dearest friends since we were children, and we have never regretted it for a moment. But Tirzah is not always an easy person to be intimate friends with. There will be more tears, more drama, than you might perhaps choose for yourself. She is very easily upset. I think if bad things happened to you – as bad things happen to all of us – she would need a lot of help to get through them. She is both very brave and very easily blown over, if that makes sense. She needs someone to love her very much and forgive her when she cannot love you as you might wish to be loved. But she is also very good at loving, almost too good. She will be my friend when I am a hundred and three, I know it, and I would consider myself a very poor sort of scoundrel indeed if I were not her friend too.

As for you . . . I cannot think of a better thing for Tirzah than to marry you. I think if you do it carefully and with as much respect for her grandmother as you can, you will change her life. But you must be sure that she is who you want before you do anything you might regret. If you abandoned her, you would break her heart. You must be very careful with her. You must keep your promises and you must forgive her mistakes. Can you do that? Do you love her that much? If you do and you can, then I think you will be very happy.

Your loving sister,

Polly

4A Ferguson Buildings
Jackson Street
Edinburgh
20th May 1897

Dear Polly,

I know it sounds foolish, after so brief a courtship, but yes. I think I do.

Your loving brother,
Michael

4A Ferguson Buildings
Jackson Street
Edinburgh
20th May 1897

Dear Tirzah,

Goodness, what a letter! I'm sorry to hear about your mother. It didn't seem exactly delicate to ask all the details when you were here, though I could see she had upset you. I can't tell you how angry it makes me to think about her treating you like that when you were such a little girl. I went so red in the face, reading your letter over breakfast, that McGovern looked quite astonished! He's rather a mild-mannered sort of chap, more interested in butterfly hunting and fishing than dipsomaniacs and runaways.

My darling Tirzah (I may call you 'my darling', mayn't I?), what happened to you was not your fault. I promise. You were a *child*. Those stories of charming baby orphans are not *real*. You know that, don't you? Just ask Polly if you don't – her orphanage is full of the most delightful orphans, all of whom deserve loving homes and gentle parents. It is not their fault that they are there, and what happened to you wasn't your fault either.

About the other thing . . . Are you sure? I have three more years of medical school, and I couldn't think of marrying before I was done. It would be a long wait, and a doctor's life is not an easy one. I don't want to be a country doctor like your grandmother's favourites – I want to be a very important specialist working in a hospital. I'm not sure what I'm going to be a specialist of quite yet, but I'm going to be very serious and important, and people are going to send their difficult cases to me, and I'll say, 'Ah, yes, young man! Clearly it's peritonitis!' and they'll all be very impressed. Doesn't that sound like a fine husband to have! But it'll be long hours and lots of work. How are you at cleaning bloodstains out of aprons?

I'm not going to ask you to marry me now. But if I *were* to ask, one day after I've graduated – what would you think of such a life as that?

Yours in rather nervous expectation,

Michael

Bannon House
Abyford
Perthshire
22nd May 1897

Darling Michael,

I would be terrible at washing blood out of aprons. Can't we send them to the laundry for that?

If you asked me to marry you, I would say yes of course, juggins. I would love to be married to a very serious and important specialist. It would be quite the thing to brag about in the drawing rooms, and all my awful old friends would want you to diagnose things for them.

Yours, if you'll have me,
Tirzah

4A Ferguson Buildings
Jackson Street
Edinburgh
24th May 1897

Dear Mrs Lewis,

I hope you will forgive my writing to you in this forward fashion. My name is Michael Anniston, and I am the gentleman who cabled you from Edinburgh on the night Tirzah went missing.

I have known Tirzah for many years – she is the dear school friend of my sister Polly and often came to stay with us in the holidays. I began writing to her after she came to Polly's eighteenth birthday party. There was nothing improper in our letters, though they were rather private. I saw no harm in writing to her, but now I think perhaps I should have asked your permission first. So here I am doing so.

I hope you will permit us to continue our correspondence. I think Tirzah is a very fine girl indeed and I hope that once I have taken my degree, in three years' time, I might have the honour of making her my wife.

Yours sincerely,
Michael Anniston

Bannon House
Abyford
Perthshire
25th May 1897

Dear Mr Anniston,

I am very grateful for your kindnesses to my granddaughter and for acting so respectfully towards her. She is much too young to consider marriage, though I would be willing for you to continue writing. However, I must ask that if she tells you of any plans to run off again, you must inform me of them at the earliest opportunity, or I may change my mind.

Yours sincerely,
Moira Lewis (Mrs)

Wimpole Street
London
25th May 1897

Dear Sebastian,

I'm sorry I have taken so long to reply to your letter. I couldn't quite work out what to say, and how to say it in a way that you would understand.

If – if – if—!

If Isabelle does not marry (she still might, you know). *If* she does another Season (not everyone does two, and certainly only a very few poor souls like Mariah do three; I am not sure Isabelle would enjoy the shame of a second Season). *If* Aunt Eliza can afford to sub another Fanshaw girl for the Season – or would even want to!

This is the desperate thing about being the poor relation. All these decisions are out of my hands. I cannot ask Aunt Eliza – I simply *cannot*. It would be unthinkable. Poor relations cannot ask for something like that. They just drop larger and larger hints, or look hopeful, until their wealthy connections present them with wonderful gifts, and then they have to be pathetically grateful all the time for the kindnesses.

I am not sure you are correct about me doing Aunt Eliza a service. Yes, I do help her out, and no, I am not paid for it; but I get my food and board, and invitations to all the best parties, and tickets to the theatre and concerts and all that. Putting a girl through a Season isn't cheap. And the understanding is that I am to repay her by marrying well, so that she is spared the expense of supporting all my younger sisters, as she does now. (Question: Does Lord St John know that he'll be paying my sisters' school fees from now on?)

So, no, I can't. Actually. Your family is shameless about asking for money, but then you're asking an actual earl. So it's rather different.

This is my life. I have thought about it, you know. It isn't so simple as it looks from the outside.

Yours despairingly,

Sophia

Royal Liverpool Home
for Orphans
Victoria Drive
Liverpool
25th May 1897

Dear Albert,

Oh, Lord.

Something has happened, and it makes me quite sick to think of it.

You remember Polly Anniston, the funny girl I have teaching my youngest children? Well, yesterday I received a visit from a woman who said that Miss Anniston had been trying to track her down!

Her name is Nora O'Flannery, and I must say, I did not think much of her. She was one of those people who start defending themselves before the attack, just to be on the safe side. She had brought her stepsons to the orphanage some months ago. I didn't like her much then either. 'Not my children, sir, just poor little orphans I wanted to do my best by, didn't want to think of them thrown out on the street with no one to care for them, now their papa is dead.'

Methinks the lady doth protest too much, as the good Danish prince said. But I just nodded away. It is no business of ours why a child ends up on our doorstep.

It took her a while to get to her grievance this time, but apparently she bumped into a woman she used to know, who told her Miss Anniston had been trying to find her! I asked her why, and she wouldn't give me a straight answer – either she did not know, or she did not want to tell me. (It could be either.) But she was outraged that Miss Anniston had been searching for her. 'I did nothing wrong, sir! Nothing at all! She is hounding me for no reason! And how did she know where we lived? Is that not confidential?'

This was a tricky one. Miss Anniston is a teacher at our school and so of course has access to all the children's records. But we care a great deal about their privacy. For a teacher to look up a child's home address and misuse that information is a serious offence. And I think Mrs O'Flannery must have seen that, because a triumphant look came over her face.

'I shall talk to Miss Anniston about it,' I promised her. 'I am sure there is a rational explanation.'

I was sure too. I couldn't see that there wouldn't be. So at break time, I summoned her to my study.

She knocked lightly on the door, and when I said 'Enter,' she came in, her whole face lighting up with pleasure to see me. It gave me a queer feeling. I think it was my first realisation – do not laugh, Albert – that perhaps something was happening here that I did not know how to manage.

I told her about Mrs O'Flannery, and at first she looked excited, then, as she realised the severity of the situation, she looked more grave.

'What explanation can you give?' I asked, for I still felt sure that she must have one.

'I can give none,' she said.

I was astonished. If you could see the grave, Quakerish way she said it, so simply and clearly. She might have fancied herself Antigone, brought before the court, willing to die for her actions.

'But . . .!' I said.

'I'm sorry,' she said. 'Oh, Mr Thompson, please believe me, I am! I do have a good reason, honour bright, I do. But I *can't* tell you what it is.'

Albert, I was flabbergasted! The truth is, the rule is that she can look at the file with a good reason but not with a bad one. Honestly, I felt like I'd wandered into one of those girls' school stories my sister was so fond of. Not a problem I often encounter in an orphanage. Polly is exactly the sort of girl who would have done jolly well at one of those schools. I can just imagine her fighting for the Honour of the School and all that rot.

The trouble is, it leaves me in a pretty dicky situation. Can I trust her word? I mean, I do trust her, I think. But can I just leave it at that?

I am almost certain that the wise headmistress in the school stories would have trusted the noble schoolgirl and been gloriously righteous when all proved explicable. But . . . oh, damn it, Albert, do I need to spell it out?

Do I want to trust this girl because I trust her, or because I am falling in love with her?

Yours wretchedly,

Theo

St Barnabas Preparatory School
Church Lane
Exeter
28th May 1897

Dear Theo,

You are a prize ass, and I cannot believe it has taken you as long as this to realise it.

For what it's worth, if you trust the girl, trust her. But do so because you trust her, not because you love her.

With barely concealed amusement,

Albert

Royal Liverpool Home
for Orphans
Victoria Drive
Liverpool
29th May 1897

Dear Albert,

You are right, of course. And yet . . . ! After the disgrace of the previous incumbent, I must strive to be entirely above board and correct. There was another affair where she did something similar – I forgave her then, rather against my better judgement. But I'm not sure I can do it again. To look the other way because I trust her is one thing. To look the other way because I wish to marry her . . . Oh, hell!

In the end, despairing over what to do next, I spoke to Miss Jessop, the head of the school. She listened gravely and said, 'Polly is a dear girl, and I am sure that whatever she did, her heart was absolutely in the right place. But just because her motives were honourable does not mean her actions were correct. We have rules for a reason. And, if I may say so, sir, I'm not comfortable with her saying she couldn't tell you. Why not?'

Oh, damn! She is right, isn't she? Damn, damn, damn!

Yours wretchedly,

Theo

St Barnabas Preparatory
School
Church Lane
Exeter
30th May 1897

Dear Theo,

Why not propose to the girl, and then the problem goes away?

Albert

Royal Liverpool Home
for Orphans
Victoria Drive
Liverpool
31st May 1897

Dear Albert,

NOT HELPFUL.

Theo

FROM: SERGEANT O'FLANNERY
MILTON BARRACKS CALCUTTA
TO: MISS ANNISTON, 45 PARK LANE
LIVERPOOL

RECEIVED YOUR LETTER STOP NO
IDEA STOP TELL BOYS I LOVE THEM
STOP
LETTER TO FOLLOW STOP SERGEANT
O'FLANNERY CALCUTTA

Flat 4, Marsh Mansions
Haydown Street
Bloomsbury
London
1st June 1897

Dear Sophia,

I know it is your life, my dear, dear, darling Sophia. But do you? You are giving up your chance of happiness because it would be impolite to take it?

I like your aunt Eliza, you know. I think she is fond of you. I think she probably understands more than you might think – she married your uncle Simon, after all. Was that for love?

You gave me two tasks, and I did them willingly enough. There are always three tasks in fairytales, but this time I think the third task should be yours. Here it is: stop trying to please everyone around you. Have the courage to take something for yourself. It is not your job to save your sisters. It is your job to live your life – the only life you have – as well and honestly as you can.

This isn't that. It's a sin – or at least it ought to be.

Ask your aunt Eliza if she'll give Louisa a Season next year. Just ask her, Sophia. Your life is worth being impolite for.

Sebastian

45 Park Lane
Liverpool
2nd June 1897

Dear Tirzah and Sophia,

Well! Great excitement in Liverpool! I have found Sergeant O'Flannery! And he is alive! And it is all as we suspected – he had no idea!

I wrote a letter to his regiment in Calcutta. I wasn't sure how long it would take to reach him, but I couldn't think what else to do. I didn't want to tell the boys in case I was wrong – but I didn't think I *was*.

Anyway, so yesterday I got a telegram from him – and he is alive! I was so excited I couldn't think. I wasn't supposed to be teaching – the children had a holiday to celebrate the birthday of the orphanage's founder – but I rushed straight up there and burst into the hall where they were at breakfast. I ran straight to the middle boys' table, where Daragh and Robert were sitting, and I showed them his telegram. Such excitement! Robert wept, and Daragh kept staring at it as though he couldn't believe it.

'It's really from my father?' he kept saying, and, 'It is! It is!' I kept laughing.

And then all the other boys on the table were crowding round, wanting to know what was happening. Lots of our children have fathers and other relations – but a father who comes back from the dead is a rare enough thing to cause a stir.

Of course, Nicholas had to be brought into the general delight. Robert and Daragh rushed off to the nursery table and showed him the telegram.

'It's from Dad!' Robert cried. 'He's alive! He's going to write to us!'

I'm not sure how much of this poor Nicholas understood, but he knew enough to know that a telegram from one's father is a grand thing.

'A telegram from my daddy!' he kept saying. And of course all the other teachers were full of exclamations and curiosity and all eager to marvel at the cruelty of the children's stepmother.

'Whatever did she think would happen when the father came home?' asked Miss Jessop.

I have been wondering about this myself. Would she even let him know where the children were? Or has she written and told him they are dead?

It frightens me just to think of it. I can't imagine being a woman like that. Can you?

I don't know what is going to happen next – and of course, it takes many weeks for a letter to come from Calcutta. But even if all that happens is that they know their father is alive and loves them – that's enough.

Yours ecstatically,

Polly

P.S. Mr Thompson was not at breakfast today. He must be ill again, poor man. I am so glad I no longer have to keep secrets from him! I do so hate lying to him, even if only by omission.

Royal Liverpool Home
for Orphans
Victoria Drive
Liverpool
2nd June 1897

Dear Miss Anniston,

I am writing to you to officially terminate your employment at the Royal Liverpool Home for Orphans. Your conduct over the past few days and your refusal to explain yourself have left me with no choice but to take this step.

In accordance with your contract, I am required to give you one month's notice; however, in light of the current circumstances, I think it best if you do not come back to work. You will be paid for your final month.

I am very sorry to have to do this; I have always considered you one of our finest employees, and I cannot imagine what can have occasioned this behaviour. I do wish you had felt able to explain yourself to me – I cannot think why you did not.

Yours sincerely,
Theodore Thompson
Superintendent

45 Park Lane
Liverpool
3rd June 1897

Dear Mr Thompson,

Please believe me, I never meant to keep secrets from you. If I could have told you what I was doing, I would have done. You cannot know how many times I've wanted to – but I couldn't. I swore to keep it secret, and I couldn't break that promise. Not to those boys. Not even for you.

But *now* I have been released. Please do let me explain it all to you. I don't ask you to give me my job back – honour bright, I don't. But I couldn't bear to think that you were out there somewhere in the world thinking ill of me.

I'll have to come in tomorrow to pick up my things. May I call on you in the morning and talk all this through?

Yours sincerely,
Polly Anniston

Royal Liverpool Home
for Orphans
Victoria Drive
Liverpool
3rd June 1897

Dear Miss Anniston,

I will be in my office between nine and eleven and will be available at your convenience.

Yours sincerely,
Theodore Thompson
Superintendent

45 Park Lane
Liverpool
5th June 1897

Dear girls,

I don't know quite how to tell you about what has happened to me. I almost don't want to tell you – in fact, I've been holding my news to myself since yesterday, keeping it close to my heart. But we're going to tell Mother and Father this evening, so . . .

I am engaged to be married.

To Mr Thompson – who I must remember to call Theo. His name is Theodore – isn't that perfect? He looks like a Theo too, all dark and clever and kind. He is so kind.

I must start my story right at the beginning. I haven't told you any of this because it's been too awful, but Mrs O'Flannery herself turned up at the orphanage apparently and complained to Mr Thompson I mean Theo – that I was harassing her! Theo called me into his office and asked why I'd been going through the children's private records. Of course I told him I couldn't say. (Honestly, it was like something out of a school story; I almost wanted to giggle. You should have seen me playing the Noble and Maligned Schoolgirl Who Will Not Betray Her Comrades. But it was awful at the same time because I could see how puzzled he was, and I hated to think that he thought badly of me. I *so* wanted to tell him the whole story – I knew he would be sensible about it. But I just couldn't.)

Anyway, he sent me away to think about it, and then we got the telegram from Sergeant O'Flannery, and there was all the excitement over that. Mr Thompson didn't know about it, because he was ill again, poor man. So I went home happy as a little bird – I wrote you both a letter telling you all about it, and took it to the post – and when I came back, there waiting for me on the hall table was a letter telling me I was dismissed.

Girls, I just froze. It was the worst thing that had ever happened to me. I wanted to run straight up to the orphanage and knock on his door – only I couldn't, of course, because he wasn't well. But I knew it was a mistake – that I could explain – that he would change his mind. He had to. The thought of never seeing the children again – never seeing *him* again . . . I kept saying, 'It can't be true. It can't be. He must listen. He must!' The little ones were all crowding around, saying, 'What's the matter, Polly?' Betsy was outraged.

And Mother said, 'You must write to him and ask to speak to him. He's a good man. He'll listen.'

So I did. I wrote him a letter and he arranged to meet me in his office – his real office, not his rooms where he does most of his business. It was very formal and awful.

I nearly put on my best dress, the one I wore for the interview, and then I thought suddenly, 'No! He's my friend.' So I didn't. I just wore my everyday skirt and blouse, the ones I wear to teach the children.

I was frightfully nervous. He sat there at his desk looking awful, but I couldn't tell if that was because he was sorry to let me go or because he'd been ill. His face was a ghastly whitish grey. I gripped my hands together and said, 'Mr Thompson, please! Please listen to me. I know I did wrong, but if you understand why – I feel sure you will forgive me.'

He rubbed his face.

'So now you can tell me,' he said. 'When your job depends on it.'

It was funny – it was almost as though I'd disappointed him by not sticking to my High-Minded Schoolgirl routine. I think I almost loved him more at that moment than I ever had before. I'd expected him to be professional and serious about it, but he wasn't. He was upset about this too.

'No,' I said. 'If I hadn't been released from my promise, I wouldn't tell you.'

He didn't answer that. He just waited. So I told him about Nicholas and Daragh and Robert. His eyes got a little wide. When I got to the part about Michael and me going to their home, he looked almost like he was trying not to laugh. When I finished, he said, 'You mean that scene yesterday morning in my dining room – that was *your* doing? I heard all about it from Annie when she brought me my tea – only by then, I'd already written to you, of course.'

'Well – yes,' I said. 'But I promised them I wouldn't tell you anything about it, so I couldn't – I just *couldn't* – you do see, don't you? They thought you were in league with her!'

He shook his head.

'Did they?' he said. 'I suppose – that awful woman was rather fawning over me. I bore it as politely as I could, but I imagine – to a child – it might have looked as though I liked it.'

'They were *sure* you were working together,' I said. 'Like something out of a Penny Dreadful.'

He shuddered. He looked rather dazed.

'Life with you is never dull, is it?' he said.

'Actually, I'm the most sensible one of my friends,' I told him. 'My friend Sophia goes to six parties and five dinners a week. She's trying to avoid an entanglement with a secretary who has a socialist sister and a monkey, but we don't think she's going to manage it. And my friend Tirzah ran away to Glasgow to find her long-lost mother and ended up stranded in Edinburgh station with no money. Going to Toxteth to look for an orphan's stepmother is tame.'

He rubbed his face. He looked tired but also amused and, I think, relieved.

'Although you aren't exactly dull yourself,' I pointed out. 'You went off to India and founded a school! That's more eccentric even than the time Tirzah and I climbed on top of the chapel roof to rescue a seagull!'

He started to laugh. He laughed and laughed and laughed and laughed.

'What?' I said. 'What's so funny?'

'Mary Anniston,' he said. 'Please marry me. I don't know how I ever imagined I could live without you.'

After that . . . Well, I'm going to draw a veil over what happened next, as they say. But we are going to live in the orphanage and run it together, and we have so many ideas! I am going to go and meet his mother next week, and we are going to get married in the chapel at the orphanage so all the children can come, and you must both come too, and oh! I am the happiest girl alive!

Yours joyfully,

Polly

Wimpole Street
London
5th June 1897

Dear Sebastian,

I hate you.
Sophia

Bannon House
Abyford
Perthshire
8th June 1897

Dear Polly and Sophia,

I knew it! I knew it! Didn't we know it, Sophia? Can we say 'I told you so' at your wedding? Can we be bridesmaids? Have you set a date? We need to meet him, you know, to judge whether he's an acceptable match. Though I must say, he sounds lovely. You will be absurdly happy, organising everything. You will have six children and never have a decent night's sleep again. Won't you just love it?

Things are – touch wood – good here too. I can't quite believe it, but it seems to be true. For one thing, we received a call from the Mackays, who live about an hour's ride away. They have a daughter a couple of years older than me, and they came to ask if I would go to tea with her next week. I am not sure how they knew I was here – perhaps Dr Brooke told them? But apparently Grandmother knew Mrs Mackay's father, and she was quite gracious and said I may go. The daughter seems nice enough. Her name is Jane. She whispered to me that she has been frightfully bored ever since her older sister got married and left home and was simply delighted to discover that I was here too.

'You must be on your very best behaviour,' Jane whispered. 'And then we may be allowed to be friends. Mother is fearfully strict, but then so is your grandmother, so I think it will be all right.'

So that is something.

For another, Grandmother got fed up of listening to me complaining about the Waverleys, and she said I could choose the next book we read! So now we are reading *A Study in Scarlet*. She keeps sniffing and saying how ridiculous it all is, but I think she is quite enjoying it. She hasn't asked me to stop, anyway.

Much love to you both. I am so happy for you, Polly, I can't tell you.

Yours affectionately,

Tirzah

Wimpole Street
London
10th June 1897

Dear Polly and Tirzah,

Oh, Polly! Like Tirzah, I am not surprised in the least, but I am very, very happy for you. I should think it is an excellent match, and you two ridiculous souls will be very happy together. (Though you are not the sensible one, darling, and you never were. You and Tirzah are quite as absurd as each other.)

And Tirzah, I am glad you and your grandmother are getting along better. I have noticed this in London too, that strict parents tend to relax once their daughters are safely engaged. Not that you and Michael are exactly engaged. But! Agatha Darling was kept so carefully that you might have thought she was made out of china. However, since her engagement, she has been allowed to go on carriage rides alone with her fiancé, and there was a rumour that they even went to a nightclub! So.

Not much news here. School has closed early, did you know? (I suppose you do, Polly.) They've all got mumps! So Mummy and Louisa have come to visit for a week. It is lovely to see them but rather fraught at the same time. I rather wish they hadn't come right now, when nothing is settled. Louisa is not yet 'out' of course – she is just sixteen and has another year yet at school – but she is being permitted to attend tea parties and tennis parties and so forth, and she is behaving very well considering her extreme youth. (Yes, I know I am only two years older, but honestly! I feel practically middle-aged compared to her. She is such a child!)

Aunt Eliza held a tea party and a dinner to celebrate our guests, and Sebastian came to both. He was a very dear fairytale hero and was very polite, talking to Mummy and generally making himself most charming and agreeable. They both loved him, of course – but who doesn't? Mummy did say to me, 'Dear, does this young man know your situation? He seems very keen.' I told her that of course he did, and she looked a little sceptical but said nothing more.

They met Lord St John and were very polite, but of course next to Sebastian, he did pall rather. It is hard to be *very* striking when you are thirty-five, with thinning hair and a bit of a paunch and an awful habit of laughing when you're nervous and can't think of anything to say. Still, Louisa seemed to do very well. She sat beside him and listened to him talking about his hunting lodge in Aberdeenshire and his house in Oxfordshire and his London residence and all the rest of it, and her eyes got bigger and bigger. Louisa might only be sixteen, but she is very mercenary. She is always wanting to know about what titles people have and how much their dresses cost and all that sort of thing. She is such a brat, but I suppose she cannot help it.

Louisa and I were sharing a bedroom, and as we were brushing our hair ready for bed, all she could talk about was how lucky I was. 'Three houses!' she said. 'A carriage and four! A title! Oh, how I wish I were you! And the worst is, you don't care a fig about any of that. Anyone can see you would rather be married to that awful little secretary. Oh, I don't mean anything by it,' she added hastily when she saw my expression. 'He's perfectly charming in his own right. But when you could be a lady!'

Huh. And to think I am doing all this for her! If she really thinks that, she can have him.

Yours, somewhat annoyed,

Sophia

45 Park Lane
Liverpool
12th June 1897

Dear Tirzah and Sophia,

Well! Whatever do you think happened today!

I was teaching the little ones – or rather, I was reading *Cinderella* to them – when a real live actual fairy godmother appeared!

No, truly. There was a knock on my door. It was one of the big girls, the student teachers, telling me to come at once to Theo's rooms. I handed her *Cinderella* and ran off at once.

There was a little woman in a red shawl sitting in an easy chair, and she jumped up as soon as I came into the room and said, 'Oh! Are you Miss Anniston? Mr Thompson has been telling me all about you, and I am *so* grateful, I can't tell you!' And she took my hands in hers and kissed me.

Her name was Mrs O'Flannery, and she was the children's grandmother, of course. She lives in a little seaside town in County Down, and Sergeant O'Flannery had sent her a telegram and she had come straight over on the ferry. She was going to take the children back to live with her until he could come home.

'He's going to try and leave the army,' she said. 'He thinks they'll be understanding of his circumstances.'

'Oh, how lovely!' I said.

'When I think of that witch of a woman! I could strangle her! To think of her writing all those letters to Eoin, sending him love from the children and telling him sweet little stories about them!'

'But what was she going to do when he came back?' I asked, because as I told you before, I've been worrying about that. I couldn't stop thinking about their poor father coming back to wherever she was living now (for of course he must know her new address) and not knowing what had happened to those little boys. Would she have told him they'd died? That was the other reason it seemed so important to find him.

'Oh! I expect they were all going to die in a cholera outbreak or something. Terribly sad. Or perhaps she wouldn't be there at all. He sent her every bit of his wages he could scrimp and save, and she was always writing with something else the boys needed: doctor's bills and new boots and so forth. Goodness knows what she really spent it on! And all the while my darling children were here, in an orphanage!'

She was such a warm, funny little woman, and I felt so glad that the boys would be going to her, at least until their father can come home. We all went down to the schoolrooms to tell them so at once. Mr Thompson – Theo, I must remember to call him – came too, for as he said, there is so much sadness in this job, we must all celebrate the joyful moments when we get them. I think that's a pretty good motto for life, personally.

The grandmother was not sure if the boys would remember her, but of course they did, and they fell on her with cries of joy. She told them to pack up their things, for they would be off that very afternoon – to her little house by the seaside, where they would all sleep snuggled up together in one big bed under the rafters and play by the sea after school. It did sound lovely. They rushed around embracing all their friends and crying, but they were happy to go, you could see it. It doesn't matter how much love you put into an orphanage – and we put in a lot – it is not the same as a grandmother and a father of your own.

Afterwards, Theo and I were rather thoughtful.

'Aren't you glad I read those files now?' I said.

'Hmm,' said Theo. 'I'm not sure I should say yes to that. What else might you consider it permission to do?'

'Oh! All sorts of things,' I said at once. 'I'm going to take the children on an excursion to New Brighton. I thought I might take the older ones camping, if we can find tents somewhere. And of course I'm going to adopt the naughtiest and the most unadoptable infants myself. How would you like to be a papa to little Bobby Flint and Davy Connell?'

‘Heaven forfend!’ he said, but he was smiling. He loves the naughty ones as much as I do – more, I think.

‘Or perhaps,’ I said, ‘you’d rather have a few little Thompsons of your own?’

‘Perhaps indeed,’ he murmured. And he pulled me to him and kissed me. And with that, my darling girls, my tale must end. For there are some things which are not to be sketched in pen and ink, though I remain,

your dear, dear friend,

Polly

Bannon House
Abyford
Perthshire
14th June 1897

Dear Polly and Sophia,

Oh, Polly, I am so glad! Everything is coming out so delightfully, isn't it?

Things are still going well here. I went over to Jane's house for tea last week. We were very formal and respectable, and sat in the drawing room with her old governess as a chaperone. It was so funny. We kept pulling faces at each other when the governess wasn't looking. And then afterwards, we went for a walk, and she introduced me to her horse, who is called Daybreak and is gorgeous. I wish I had a horse. Jane is in love with a boy called James, whom she danced with at her sister's house. She was very impressed when I told her about Michael. I like her a lot, but not nearly as much as I like you two.

Grandmother enjoyed *A Study in Scarlet* so much we are now reading *The Sign of the Four*. She likes to guess who did it and how, and I take great delight in telling her she's wrong. (She always is.) She doesn't seem to mind.

Michael remains divine. He is writing me two letters a week now, and Grandmother doesn't even blink. We are not engaged, although we *have* talked about it. He wants to wait until he has graduated, and Grandmother thinks this is very sensible. Would you ever have believed that you two would be married at eighteen (I know you are not engaged yet, Sophia, but you will be soon if Lord St John has anything to do with it), and I would be sensibly waiting until my beloved was financially settled? But I think it is very good for me to have a sensible husband, since I am so foolish myself. You two are both practical enough to run your own households. I never thought I'd say this, but I think I need to grow up a bit first. I don't mind waiting.

Yours, very sensibly,

Tirzah

Wimpole Street
London
15th June 1897

Dear girls,

Well! You will not believe what has happened! My fairytale hero has done it! I am engaged! And oh! I never thought I could ever be so happy!

It is all down to Louisa.

I told you, didn't I, that she was jealous of me marrying Lord St John, of all the foolish things? She went on and on and on, and eventually I lost my temper. 'Well!' I said. 'If you feel like that, why don't *you* marry him? I'm sure I don't want to!'

She stared at me.

'But isn't he in love with you?' she said.

I had to laugh. Was *I* so naive when I started the Season?

'Lord St John wants a pretty young wife to hang off his arm and run his shooting parties for him. He knows he stands no chance of catching one of the heiresses, so he's picked me. I'm a practical choice – I'm pretty enough, well-educated, and not afraid of a bit of hard work. And I can't be too picky about looks or personality. Not that I'm sure he puts it quite like that – but he must know he's hardly an Adonis.'

I'm not sure he knows how I feel about him – he is not very observant – but if Louisa really *did* want him . . .

Louisa assured me she did. 'I like him,' she said. 'And I never wanted a grand love affair, you know. I just want – oh! To have my own home. To never be dependent on wealthy relations again. *You* know.'

So we settled it between us.

For the last five days, when Lord St John came by, Louisa would sit beside him and take his hand. She would ask him about Scotland, and his houses, and say 'Oh, I *wish* I could see them!' and they would talk about horses and hunting and things. I thought she was horribly forward and obvious, but she *is* only sixteen, and Lord St John seemed flattered. I suppose it must be rather nice to be so obviously feted.

Meanwhile, clever Sebastian seemed to have noticed what was going on. *He* decided to stake his claim to me with the brightest, biggest flag he could find. Every day, while Louisa was sitting by Lord St John, he would come and sit by me and tell me stories about the children, and the parties he was organising for Lord Winterbourne. He was quite right – he is a good secretary. (I am always invited to every party Lord Winterbourne hosts. I am not sure Lord Winterbourne knows this, but it is jolly good fun all the same.) He wouldn't say anything out loud, but it simply became more and more obvious to everyone in the room that I was Sebastian's and Louisa was Lord St John's.

Yesterday was the final night of Louisa's stay. Lord St John held a dinner party, and we were all invited (though not Sebastian). He placed Louisa next to him and myself at the other side of the room, which I thought was hopeful, and they spent the whole evening whispering to each other. It did make me feel queer, watching them. Not because I'm jealous – she is welcome to him – but because Louisa is *so* young, and he is so, well, middle-aged. And it got me wondering how *I* must have looked when I sat beside him and nodded away at his conversation. And it just made me so *sad* for all the girls sent out to the marriage market, sold off to the highest bidder, all of us fresh out of the schoolroom. I know I have escaped it, but I so very nearly didn't.

I loved our school, as you know, but I do wish sometimes that Miss Clearly had prepared us more for modern life. We learned no science, not even any Latin or Greek, so none of us could ever go to university. None of us were remotely fit for any sort of profession, besides teaching. I can play the piano well enough, and converse in French, I have a good grounding in English literature, and a moderate grounding in mathematics. I can name my kings and queens of England and the great rivers of the world. But suppose I were to have a burning desire to be a doctor or a lawyer or some sort of businesswoman – how would I even begin to go about it? It just seems such a *waste*! When I think of asses like Sebastian (and though I love him dearly, he *is* an ass) who fill the universities, and clever, sensible sorts like Polly, who cannot even take a degree, it makes my blood boil!

Well. I digress. But there really is very little more to tell. Lord St John proposed to Louisa, Louisa said yes. Sebastian came round the next day and heard all and begged to be allowed to marry me. Mummy – who is no fool – agreed. Lord St John will support my sisters. I shall marry Sebastian. Louisa will be a lady. I shall be poor but happy, with my dear, darling, absurd husband. Oh! The things we shall do! We shall have a dog and a cat. And a little garden. We shall have a maid but not much more than that. But we've already agreed between us that I shall learn to type, which is, after all, a respectable profession, and I can hardly fail to find work. Sebastian's mother and father are to give me a typewriter as a wedding present – did you ever hear of anything so ridiculous?

Your joyful, practical, and romantic friend,

Sophia

P.S. Little brother Tobias says his wedding present is going to be a parrot. Do you think it will talk?

Dear Polly,

Just a short P.S. to ask – what do you *really* think about Michael and Tirzah? Do you think she loves him or has she just grabbed the first man who wandered across her line of sight?

And what about Michael? Does he love her? Will they be happy, do you think?

I know I should be pleased – and it does have all the trappings of the happy ending – the handsome prince, the noble rescue, etc, etc. But I can't help but worry. Tirzah is not very discriminating, as you know. What do you think?

Your sensible friend,

Sophia

45 Park Lane
Liverpool
17th June 1897

Dear Tirzah and Sophia,

Oh, Sophia! How wonderful! Goodness, it is like the last scene of a farce, isn't it, with us all getting engaged left, right, and centre? Who's going to be next? Will Tirzah's grandmother run off with the curate, or Isabelle marry Tobias? Find out all in next month's edition of *Household Words*!

In all seriousness, I could not be more delighted. I put forward myself immediately for bridesmaid duties, especially if your aunt Eliza is buying the bridesmaid dresses.

I have news too, though it's nowhere near as exciting as yours. We reported the wicked stepmother to the police, but we never expected them to do anything about it. I wasn't even sure whether she'd committed a crime or not – is it illegal to put someone else's children in an orphanage? I mean, if she really was unable to care for the children, she would have been entirely within her rights to use us. And lying to your husband isn't a crime. Is it?

But I needn't have worried. It turns out Mrs O'Flannery is not Mrs O'Flannery at all. In fact, she's a professional bigamist! She is, according to the policeman who came to the orphanage, married to six different men all at the same time!

Most of the men, like Sergeant O'Flannery, are serving overseas, either in the army or the colonies or both, and she made quite a tidy living on the various pay packets they sent home to her. The children were an unusual addition, but I suppose she always intended to get rid of them one way or the other. She was absolutely unrepentant, apparently. I suppose it is quite a clever way to go about things, although how she managed when two of her husbands had leave at the same time, one can only imagine!

Anyway, she has now been arrested, but more importantly, it means that she and Sergeant O'Flannery were never married! So he can marry again if he chooses. I got a letter from him last week; he has been granted emergency discharge from the army and is going to come home and live with his mother, and they will raise the children together.

The orphans' school breaks up next week, which means I am free for the summer! My brothers and sisters are all home now too and we are going to the Isle of Man for a month! I cannot wait! Sophia, do you think there is any chance you might be able to join us, even for a week? Tirzah, I believe my mother asked your grandmother if you could come, and she said no, but perhaps now you are nearly engaged to Michael, she might reconsider . . . ?

Oh! I am so happy! Isn't everything glorious?

Your delighted friend,

Polly

45 Park Lane
Liverpool
17th June 1897

Dear Sophia,

I sent a long letter with proper congratulations, but as that will have to go through Tirzah first, here are some early congratulations to add to the heap. You don't need me to tell you, I hope, how very very pleased I am.

I know what you mean about Tirzah. I can't *not* worry, especially when the two sides of the marriage contract are two of the dearest people in the world to me.

I talked to Mother about it, and she said nothing can happen until Michael is qualified – which will not be for years, you know. Michael will be certain to meet women in that time, and she will make sure to invite Tirzah here for holidays – not with the express purpose of introducing her to men, naturally, but to make certain she knows she has options. I shall of course invite her to stay with Theo and me, and you and Sebastian must do the same.

If we can give her real choices, I think she is astute enough to know that she can take them. And I do genuinely think she loves Michael. Michael certainly loves her. As to whether it will last – well! Who can say?

One thing I can say without hesitation is that Michael will not compel her to marry him if he knows that she is unhappy. And she would certainly release him if he wished to be released. You know that as well as I. So I think we must hope, and love them as well as we can, and trust that all will be well. I think it has a good chance of working out. Michael is kind and dear and very loving, which is exactly what Tirzah needs. I am certain his regard is genuine. I think it has as much chance as our own engagements. And who can say better than that?

Yours hopefully,

Polly

Bannon House
Abyford
Perthshire
19th June 1897

Dear Polly and Sophia,

SOPHIA! THIS IS THE BEST NEWS I EVER HEARD! Please have an enormous grand wedding in St George's, Hanover Square, and invite Polly and me! Aunt Eliza or Louisa can pay for it. And please invite the monkey.

Yours, delighted,
Tirzah

P.S. I asked my grandmother about the Isle of Man. She didn't say yes, but she didn't say no . . .

Wimpole Street
London
21st June 1897

Dear Polly and Tirzah,

Thank you for your good wishes. I cannot believe it either! Yes, of course you may both be bridesmaids. My sisters are going to be bridesmaids too, though not Louisa, as she is to be married first. A quiet wedding in the chapel at Lord St John's house in Aberdeenshire, apparently. *We* are to be married in London, as Sebastian is dearest friends with half of London Society, all of whom must apparently be invited. Heaven knows how we shall pay for it all, but between Daddy, Uncle Simon, the earl and Louisa, I expect we shall manage. I cannot wait!

All is very busy here. Everyone is leaving London and going to the country. (Even people like Sebastian who live here always are apparently going to spend the summer at shooting parties and things at people's houses. Not that Sebastian actually likes shooting, but that isn't the point. Don't ask me. I don't pretend to understand these people.) Anyway, Aunt Eliza and Uncle Simon are busy packing up the house ready to go home. Mariah is going to be married next month, as Ralph is eager to get back to America. Preparing a trousseau for a woman who is going to live on a ranch is not something they cover in *The Lady*, let me tell you! But everyone is wildly excited about the whole thing, and Aunt Eliza has been quizzing Ralph and other Americans constantly, and really, it is rather wonderful.

Poor old Mummy doesn't have the first idea what to do about Louisa and me; she doesn't have nearly enough money for all the things Louisa will need, and even Sebastian, though he seems so eccentric, turns out to have the oddest ideas about what is required. The more time I spend with the upper classes, the more strange they appear. I am leaving him and Mummy and Louisa to sort it out between them.

Sebastian and I are going on our honeymoon to New York in the autumn. It is all decided. Lord Winterbourne is going there for the summer, and he is taking Sebastian as his secretary – of course – and he has agreed to let me come along too. New York! Can you imagine? I keep pinching myself. I am going back home for a few weeks to see Mummy and Daddy and the girls, but Mummy said I can come to the Isle of Man for a week, Polly. Oh, I cannot wait to see you again! I have so much to tell you that cannot be put in a letter.

I am so happy, girls. I don't think I'd realised until Louisa and Lord St John got engaged how wretched I'd been feeling. I'd just pushed the part of me that wanted something else to one side and pretended it didn't matter. But it *did* matter, and now that part of me can have what she wants – oh! How happy she is.

When I get my little house with Sebastian, I am going to sing and sing all day long. We shall have sensible daughters – one is going to be a mathematician, one a lawyer, and one a doctor, we are quite decided. I'll send them to co-educational schools, so when they come out, they can earn their living if they choose. They will never be beholden to a man.

I'm so happy, girls, I can't tell you. I feel like I've been set free. Sebastian has made me promise to take a holiday from being sensible for a full month after we are married, and I must say I think it might be the best idea I've ever heard. He is not such a foolish boy as he looks, you know, and I am your dear, loving friend,

Sophia

Bannon House
Abyford
Perthshire
23rd June 1897

Dear Mrs Anniston,

My apologies for the tone of my previous letter. I was naturally very upset at Tirzah's disobedience and so not in a state of mind to accept what I saw as chastisements. After some consideration, however, I have decided that it may be beneficial for my granddaughter to spend some time with other young people. I have therefore decided to accept your invitation for her to spend the summer with you and your family.

If you could furnish me with details of trains, dates, addresses, etc., I would be extremely grateful.

I remain, your obedient servant,

Moira Lewis (Mrs)

45 Park Lane
Liverpool
24th June 1897

Dear Sophia and Tirzah,

Tirzah! My mother just got your grandmother's letter! I never shrieked so loud in all my life! You are coming to the Isle of Man with us! Though goodness, your grandmother does like to cut things fine, doesn't she? You have a week to make your preparations! Make sure she buys you a bathing-dress – and a parasol – and a new summer hat! Oh! And you will need good boots for walking, and make sure you have plenty of warm underwear, as the house gets rather chilly even in summer.

Oh, it will be so jolly to have you with us, I can't tell you! And if you come, Tirzah, I am sure Michael will too. He was hemming and hawing between coming with us and going trekking across France with some awful undergraduates, but I am sure you will change his mind! And Theo said he would try to come across for a week. I had to bully him into taking a holiday, but of course the trustees agreed at once. He considers himself entirely indispensable, bless him!

Yours in excited haste,

Polly

Willow House
Little Glebeford
Derbyshire
25th June 1897

Dear Sebastian,

Well, I am home. Everyone is very excited to see me – which is very sweet of them, since Louisa's is the proposal which is really headline news. I am just a note in the Announcements column. But I think Mummy and Louisa must have been telling them about you, because they are all fiendishly curious. Which is nice.

I know it's only been a day, but I do miss you. I'm rather surprised at myself. I didn't think I would, somehow. I've got used to seeing you every day, and I'm not at all the romantic sort who swoons at the sound of your name. But after months and months of feeling like an odd shoe at Aunt Eliza's house, I find I have rather grown out of the home I left behind, and now I'm an odd shoe here as well. It's most disconcerting. I wish you were here; you are probably the only person who would understand what I mean. You're a very understanding sort.

There's something I need to tell you. I wasn't going to. I didn't want you to think you'd won. But then it felt unfair not to, somehow, when you'd been so faithful. So I will.

I did do it. Talk to Aunt Eliza. I wasn't going to – you haven't the first notion how difficult it is to get a minute alone with another person in that house at the height of the Season. We were always going somewhere or doing something or else rushing about having hysterics.

But there was one day – when everyone had gone out to the theatre. Aunt Eliza had a headache. So I said I would stay and read to her instead. If you ask me, she was grateful to have someone else to do the chaperoning for a change. It is hard work, being a chaperone.

It was a dreadfully rainy night, and we both felt grateful to be inside, listening to the rain slooshing down the gutters. I read to her for a while, then she looked across at me and said, 'You're a dear girl, Sophia. I will miss you.'

It seemed unlikely I would ever get such a chance again. Truly, Sebastian, I felt as though God had set her down before me and was saying 'Go on, then. If you want it, take it.' So I cleared my throat and said, 'Aunt. If – if I do not find a husband—'

She looked rather amused. 'I don't think that is very likely, do you?'

I blushed. 'If I do not find a wealthy husband, then—'

She stiffened. She knew what I was talking about. She knew how you feel about me, of course. I should think everyone did.

'Yes?'

'Well – I just—' I stammered. It seemed so appalling a thing to ask for. She spends so much money on me! 'If – well, if Isabelle does another Season, then – I mean, there's Louisa, and – well—' I trailed off. 'I suppose it wouldn't be possible,' I said. 'I'm not – I don't mean to demand. I just—'

I stopped. I never felt so ashamed in all my life. I hate asking for things. I hate it more than anything. I've always liked being someone who gives, perhaps because my sisters and I have had to accept so much from others. And although I hated being a charity case, I didn't feel like one, because I was helping my sisters. I was sacrificing *my* happiness for theirs.

I know you'll think it queer, but it felt easier giving my life away than taking it for myself. Taking meant taking from Aunt Eliza – who has been so good to me. As it happened, Louisa was much more suited to marrying for money than I was – or marrying Lord St John anyway. But of course I didn't know that then. I just felt like I was putting my own happiness above my sisters' – which is a horrible thing to do. Yet I suppose my parents put their happiness above mine – if they hadn't married for love, I wouldn't have had to marry for money. But then if they hadn't married for love, I wouldn't be here at all, I suppose.

Aunt Eliza was looking at me in a way she never had before – as though she were realising for the first time what I was being asked to do.

'Of course, if you don't want to, that's all right,' I said. I couldn't look at her. 'I just – I just thought, well . . . It's my life,' I said helplessly. 'My whole life, and—'

'I didn't know things had gone so far with you and Mr Fowler,' she said quietly. 'I thought it was just a flirtation.'

I could feel my face going scarlet. I didn't know what to say. But I didn't need to.

'Isabelle may yet find a match,' she said.

'Yes – yes, of course—' I said quickly.

'And your parents may not give consent.'

'No, but . . .'

I looked up at her, trying to show everything I felt in my eyes. I kept thinking about Uncle Simon. I know they are not happy together. Does she love him? I never thought of my aunts and uncles being actual human beings with personalities before. But they are, of course.

Aunt Eliza shook her head. 'I'm not sure I'd want to ally my fortunes with a man like Mr Fowler,' she said. 'His family spend their lives lurching from one catastrophe to another.'

'I know,' I said quietly. My family do too, in a less dramatic way. It's what I'm used to, though I can't pretend I enjoy it. I always thought I'd marry someone more stable.

'This job of his is very quaint,' she said. 'But do you expect him to still be a secretary in thirty years' time?'

'I can work too,' I said quickly.

'That's all very well until you have a child,' she said, and I bit my lip, because I do want children – tremendously. Not immediately, of course – but one day.

'I expected you to choose more sensibly,' she said. 'But naturally, if we were to do another Season, I wouldn't desert your family.'

I sat there, looking at my hands. I was trembling. I could see it – so clearly – how I could just hand it all back to them, the duty, the obligation, the responsibility. I could just walk out of the door and go to your house and say 'I'm yours'.

Aunt Eliza was looking at me again with that strange expression.

'I've resented my family my whole life,' she said, very quietly. 'They wanted me to marry well, and I didn't want to let them down. But you know, if I'd chosen differently, I think the guilt might have been easier to live with than the resentment.'

I couldn't look at her.

'I'm frightened of being poor,' I said. She nodded.

'That, I do understand.'

Oh, Sebastian. I don't know what I would have chosen if Louisa hadn't saved me. I don't know if I'd have married you. But I think – I'm almost sure – I wouldn't have married Lord St John.

I'm so glad that choice was taken away from me.

I love you. More than I think you know. I'll see you Saturday. Come quickly.

Your very own,

Sophia

Bannon House
Abyford
Perthshire
28th June 1897

Dear Polly and Sophia,

I am sitting on my windowsill, looking out over the garden. It's not such a bad view on a day like today. I can see the mountains in the distance, and smoke rising over the village. There's a lot to like here.

I had a letter from Michael this morning. He is well and sends his love.

This afternoon, I am going dress shopping with Grandmother. She said that since I had spent all my money on gallivanting about, I would clearly need more for a summer wardrobe. She's right; I hadn't thought about that. I am to have two new frocks, and two new bonnets, and a parasol. And this evening we are to have the curate over for a musical evening. The musical evening will be dire but the curate is cheerful enough. I am going to spend all evening seeing how many times I can make him blush. Grandmother will look disapproving, but she will think it is funny really.

Grandmother is a lot easier to live with now I am almost engaged to a handsome young medical student from Liverpool. Do tell Michael how grateful I am.

It's nearly dinnertime, so I must go and dress. I nearly forgot what I meant to say in this letter, which is thank you – thank you – thank you. Thank you for being my friends. Sophia, I remember the very first time I met you. You were standing in the doorway in a white silk party dress with a blue sash. You were determined that you would wear your best dress for your first day of school, and all the other girls were laughing at you. But I thought you looked lovely, and I came over to you and put my arm in yours and whispered in your ear, 'You look like a fairy princess.' And you gave me the most dazzling smile – I can still remember it now – and said, 'I *am* a fairy princess.' And right at that moment I knew we were going to be friends. And we were – the best of friends, just the two of us, until the day Polly arrived. You didn't look like a princess at all, Polly, with your hair in two fat pigtails and a book in your lap. You were sitting in the window seat in our bedroom – we had a new bedroom that year – and you said, 'Don't talk to me; I've just got to a good bit,' and you made us wait until you'd finished the chapter before you looked at us. Sophia was inclined to giggle, but I rather liked it. I liked storybooks too, and I liked how determined you were. I knew we would be friends too.

Girls, I sometimes think your friendship saved my life. Without you I would be quite alone – Grandmother doesn't count; she's too newly a person to truly be part of my life, and I cannot quite trust that she really does care for me yet. You're the closest thing to a family I have. Thank you – thank you!

I love you.

Your friend,

Tirzah

Acknowledgements

I've wanted to write an epistolary novel for years, partly because the practical challenges appealed to me, and partly because of how much I loved Jaclyn Moriarty's Ashbury/Brookfield books. They're well worth a read if you enjoy this format.

E. M. Delafield is best known for *The Diary of a Provincial Lady*, but her semi-autobiographical account of the Victorian Season, *Consequences*, was both desperately sad and fantastically useful. Nancy Mitford's *Love in a Cold Climate* and *The Pursuit of Love* are set thirty years later, but have inspired many a novel of the Season, this one included. For both a well-executed epistolary novel and an exploration of turn-of-the-century ideas around orphanages, Jean Webster's *Dear Enemy* was enlightening. Sallie's instincts around child-rearing are surprisingly modern, although her opinions of some of the children she is in charge of are alarmingly eugenic. The Museum of Liverpool's recreation of a slum courtyard made a late-stage appearance as the O'Flannery children's home. And for a general account of a late Victorian girlhood, Gwen Raverat's *Period Piece* and M. V. Hughes' *A London Child of the 1870s*, *A London Girl of the 1880s* and *A London Home in the 1890s* were fascinating.

Fairy tales are of course a running theme too: particular thanks go to Giambattista Basile's Petrosinella and Hans Christian Andersen's 'The wild swans.' You will probably spot some other fairy tale influences too, although I was halfway through the manuscript before I realised I had given Sophia a Fairy Godmother and two Ugly Stepsisters.

Female friendship is a strong theme in late Victorian and Edwardian writing for girls, and a tradition I'm proud to continue. I thought a lot about my friends Nicola, Carolyn and Sarah when writing this book, and about how young women support each other through emotional upheaval and the complexities of early adult life. I'm so grateful I knew you as a teenager and now. Thank you for being my friends.

Thanks to Katy Moran for suggesting I write about 'messy victorian teenage girls and all their drama'. How could I resist? Thanks, as ever, to my husband Tom, for being so supportive and understanding of this ridiculous career choice. Thanks to my wonderful agent Jodie Hodges and my editors Charlie Sheppard in the UK and Susan Van Metre in the US. Particular thanks to both of you for flagging all my many continuity errors, and for suggesting that Sebastian's letters should also appear. You were so right. Thanks to the Placers for general writerly support. And thanks to everyone who has read and championed my books. I couldn't do this without you.

THINGS A BRIGHT GIRL CAN DO

SALLY NICHOLLS

It's 1914, and women still have no vote. Evelyn is rich and clever, but she isn't allowed to go to university. She wants freedom and choice, even if it means paying the highest price alongside her fellow Suffragettes. Meanwhile, May campaigns tirelessly for women's votes with other anti-violence suffragists. When she meets Nell, a girl who's grown up in hardship, the two start to dream of a world where all kinds of women can find their place. But the fight for freedom will challenge Evelyn, May and Nell more than they ever could imagine. As the Great War looms, just how much are they willing to sacrifice?

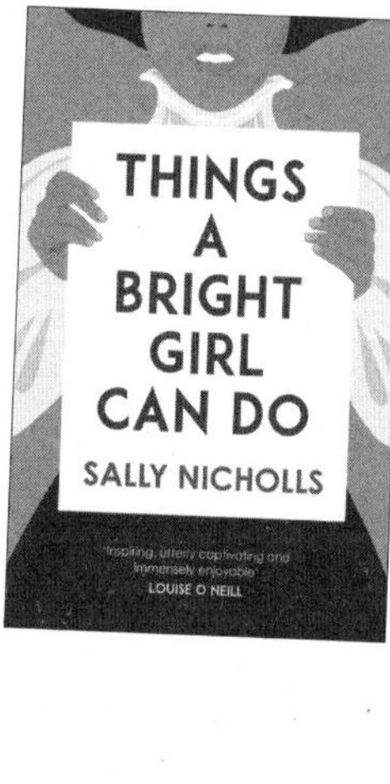

'Fantastic . . . vivid, hard-hitting, funny and emotionally compelling'
Frances Hardinge

'Nicholls has brought alive the young women of the past to empower the next generation'
The Times